The Spirit Guides

By Phoebe Garnsworthy

Also By Phoebe Garnsworthy:

Lost Nowhere: A Journey Of Self-Discovery (Book 1 of 2)

Lost Now Here: The Road To Healing (Book 2 of 2)

Daily Rituals: Positive Affirmations To Attract Love, Happiness And Peace

www.PhoebeGarnsworthy.com

The Spirit Guides/ Phoebe Garnsworthy -- 1st ed.
ISBN-13: 978-0-9954119-1-3

Dedication

This book is dedicated to the Spirits who guide us.
To those who stay by our side and encourage us to fulfill our
spiritual contract that we signed before we were born. Your
love never goes unnoticed, it is appreciated and honored with
eternal gratitude.

Contents

One

Secrets Between Sisters

"I don't know the answers either." Chloe whispered to the puppy as he lifted his head. His floppy ears hung low to the table and he tilted his left one closer to her as though he was truly listening.

"Everything's confusing me." she whispered, as she reflected on her life.

She felt tormented from trying to make a decision, hopelessly lost about which life path to take. Her mind was overloaded with endless possible outcomes as each choice was presented to her. She had no idea which was the right one that served her best. Should she choose a boring career path that made good money, or something that she was truly passionate about? Each probability held a glimmer of hope that perhaps it could be the right direction to take, but how would she ever really know?

"How do I know if I'm making the right decision?" Chloe sighed in her mind, telepathically feeling as though the puppy could hear her. The dog's blue eyes stared at her with anticipation. A feeling of hope and despair merged together into one emotion and she empathized with the small puppy, who she somehow knew was feeling the same way.

"I know, I know." she cooed soothingly, as she patted his soft brown fur on the tip of his head just above his eyes and massaged the skin that rolled over his teeth and along his jawline prompting him to close his eyes with pleasure. In that moment of nurturing love and support the puppy's entire energy changed; he forgot about the pain he was feeling and took a great big breath, sighing with comfort and relief for the connection that he felt with Chloe, one that he had sought after for so long.

"What's wrong with this one Ashley? He just seems so sad?" Chloe asked, turning to her sister who was listening to the heartbeat of a white dog on the veterinarian's table.

"He is sad." Ashley frowned back. "His owners haven't given him enough attention, so his medicine literally is just to be loved and cuddled."

"To be loved and cuddled?" Chloe echoed back with disbelief and hurt, wondering how someone could neglect the responsibility to give the love that they had once chosen.

"It sounds so simple. How could someone not love you!" Chloe continued to talk to the puppy as she wrapped her arms tightly around his body and she stroked his fur with long fluid strokes from the tip of his neck down to his belly. The puppy nuzzled his face into Chloe's arms, and a soft wheezing breath breezed through his nose.

"Isn't it beautiful though?" Chloe said as she patted the fur of the puppy's throat. "That no matter how neglected these animals feel, their faith is not broken. And they give themselves wholeheartedly to their next owner, even though they too could potentially break their heart."

Ashley stopped what she was doing.

"Whoa Chloe, that was a bit deep. Are we talking about the dogs here, or your own love life right now?" she smirked.

"Ugh. I don't even think that it's my love life that's bothering me! I think I'm just overwhelmed with all these decisions to make and I just can't make them. Do I go on a date with Tom and risk getting hurt again? But even so, I don't even think that's the real problem here."

"You don't?"

Chloe quickly shook her head.

"No, I think I'm just putting off the real issue. Like, what am I going to do after I finish school?" She looked to her sister with tears in her eyes, the confusion of being unable to make a decision had resulted in the emotion of sadness from a feeling of inadequacy at being unable to decide her true path's calling. She felt as though her inability to make a choice presented herself as weak, as she was continuously asking others for answers to her questions that no one could answer but herself. She patted the puppy again.

"You're coming to the party with me tonight?" her sister teased, knowing perfectly well that Chloe didn't mean what was she going to do after school literally that day.

"Ashley! I'm serious. Everyone has got plans, like: study for 4 years, get a job, or go traveling. I have nothing. NOTHING. No passion, no direction, just NOTHING. Oh, this sucks."

Ashley stopped feeding the puppy and came closer to her sister. She lifted Chloe's chin and stared her squarely in the eyes, and she held her gaze here for several seconds, ensuring that their breath was relaxed and in sync.

"Please listen to me carefully, Chloe. You, my friend, are in THE most exciting time of your life! You are two years away from being an adult which means you get to play in the teenager realm just a little bit longer before all the responsibilities set in and on top of that -you get to choose what you want to do! - Not many people have that choice. Chloe, do you know how lucky you are?" her voice trailed off as she looked up to the ceiling, imagining the same feeling she'd had only a few years ago. "You can do absolutely anything you want to in this world. Absolutely anything you set your mind to. Now stop playing the victim and allow the decision to come to you when the time is right."

Chloe glared at her sister. She hated being told that she was playing the victim and hated even more when Ashley pulled the older sister card and acted all high and righteous. But, sadly, she couldn't really argue with her this time and respectfully agreed with her.

"Okay, you are right." Chloe said slowly, rolling her eyes in resignation. "So what do I do now?"

"Of course I'm right." Ashley winked as she took the puppy out from Chloe's hands and replaced it with her school bag. "Now go home and meditate on it." she continued, as she pushed Chloe toward the front door. "Clear your mind and just enjoy the feeling of not knowing. Don't try and change it to be anything else but this. You are meant to be feeling this way." she said as she tapped Chloe on the shoulder and opened the back door. Chloe stood there, not wanting to walk through.

"And then what?" Chloe asked like a little child who enjoyed being told what the game was and how to play it.

"Get a journal, write down your thoughts and feelings and just keep writing until you can't write anymore, and somewhere in that mix of chaotic thoughts you will find your answer. I promise you."

"And if not?" Chloe stood in the doorway pleading to be saved. She clung to her school bag in her hand with one foot out the door and drooped her eyes low, feeling a dark depression starting to swallow her thoughts whole. She could feel the pressure from her parents on her shoulders even though they weren't next to her. And although they said they would support whatever career path she chose, it was difficult to compete with her beautiful, smart sister who had devoted her life to saving animals. She would never aspire to be something so courageous.

"Look, if you feel this lost, perhaps you need to ask your Spirit Guides?" Ashley said, casually shrugging her shoulders and delivering the question as though it were a normal suggestion.

"My Spirit Guides?" Chloe's eyes sparkled with excitement, feeling a slight sense of salvation with a new ritual that would help her find answers to her future path.

Chloe had always been interested in the supernatural, and had wasted far too much money on psychics over the years. Every experience was basically the same. She walked in, was told a bunch of stuff that she already knew about herself, was given false hope about things that couldn't possibly come true, and left, feeling like she had just been scammed. But still, every six months she heard a tip about a new psychic in town that took months to get to see, and who sounded like the real thing. But nope, it was just another time waster.

"Yeah, wait, you've never met your Spirit Guides?" Ashley replied in disbelief, for she was sure she had told her sister about them before.

"Umm . . . Ashley, what do you mean? You've never told me about the Spirit Guides!" Chloe retorted with her hands on her hips. She was irritated that her sister had been keeping this secret from her, a secret that sounded like it could potentially be the answer to all of her questions!

"Ohh, I went through a stage of talking to them a lot, when Brent and I broke up."

It was the first time Ashley had mentioned his name without her lips quivering. And she wasn't staring off into the distance like a wounded child as she was talking about their breakup. Chloe couldn't help but feel slightly guilty when Ashley mentioned his name. She had seen Brent and his new girlfriend at the movies only yesterday, but she didn't want to tell her sister. What was the point? It was just information that would hurt her again now that she was finally getting better. It was eight months since their breakup and at last she was able to shrug it off as an experience that made her grow. She didn't even define it as bad anymore. It was perhaps, "unfortunate", or "misleading", but no, not bad.

"How can it have been bad when I was fortunate enough to be able to feel such a deep love for someone?" Ashley would say. "It was beautiful to feel love like that. And now I understand why it ended. Because I needed to feel the hatred too. I needed to feel the full weight of its opposite, I needed it in order to know both sides, to be able to understand the emotion I was feeling." she explained to Chloe one day after she had literally healed herself with time spent in nature and reading inspirational books. She was always learning, endlessly learning. "She was born with glasses ready for reading books" their father had joked. And as for Chloe . . . Well, she was the artistic sister. Her emotions and creativity overrode each other, like the chaotic madness of lightning and thunder in a stormy sky. Together, they created a powerful and destructive force. Her creative passions demanded her time, erupting as an emotional release. It was the same way that thunder needed lightning in order to be created, her artistic energy didn't flow unless she felt the weight of a strong emotional inspiration to prompt a release. They swallowed each other whole and then spat each other out. First one and then the other in an ongoing violent dance of emotion and creativity. It was beautifully poetic, but of course the emotions could get the better of her, overtake her mind and lead her into an ultimate low of suffering.

When Chloe painted an empathetic picture of the sadness she had felt for her sister, the lines appeared to swirl into a never-ending hole of black and grey with tiny slithers of white, a white that was compressed and suffocated by the darkness around it. Chloe remembered trying to explain the painting without really knowing where the words had come from, and that Ashley was allowing the darkness to override her love. She believed that Ashley's mind was turning from love to fear, fear that love would never come to her again. But that was the way that Chloe painted. She never understood what came over her, but her body on its own took on a new form. A magical trance-like state existed between Chloe and her brush while the delicious textured paint swept across the blank canvas.

One day Ashley said to Chloe. "I still remember just seeing black, and I asked you, 'Why did you paint a black painting for me?' And then as I slowly got better, I saw the white and it made me laugh because it was so clear that I was surprised I had never seen it before. It's amazing how the mind only sees what it wants to see."

Chloe thought back to the painting, and how strong her creative desire was to be expressed. She compared it to how stuck she now felt. The inability to make a decision held her down and confined her to a small box. She couldn't seem to break through it and as a result, her creativity was impossible to find.

"Talk to your Spirit Guides, they will help you." Ashley soothed, patting her sisters back lovingly. "I'm telling you Chloe, it will be a positive influence on whatever the problem is you are feeling at the moment."

Ashley nodded with encouragement, understanding her sister well. With only three years apart in age, the two were inseparable. They were deeply connected together; feeling the same emotion, or worse, they would rub the emotion of one onto the other, to the extent that when one sister felt depressed the other would also fall into a pit of depression.

But the feeling Chloe was now experiencing was different from depression. It was fear of the future, a form of anxiety. Such an awful feeling: an unsettling mixture of anticipation and worry which had now physically manifested into nervous energy that shifted through her body like a ping pong ball, moving quickly and unpredictably. It crept up into her mind when she least expected it and took charge of her emotions and her rational mind.

It was difficult for Chloe to define this feeling. Often it was just an empty space surrounding her thoughts. Endless questions, constant worry as to why the questions were unable to be answered, her fear of making the wrong decision taking over. This fear then triggered the emotion of sadness to overwhelm her, propelling tears to wash over her face. But little did she know that those tears were actually cleansing her essence so that a new and improved version of herself could be created. They were creating the opening for an empty, hallow shell at her core, one that could be filled with her own potion of beauty.

"I'm feeling like there's a glass door in front of me, and behind that door is what I need to do, but for some reason, I just won't open my eyes." Chloe sighed to Ashley, irritated and frustrated with her own attitude.

"They will open that door for you." Ashley replied.

"Who will?"

"Your Spirit Guides. They are here to guide you on your life's path. If you feel lost, they will show you the way." Ashley said, smiling with reassurance.

"Okay, tell me how to do it." Chloe asked as she put her school bag down. It was always too heavy; she didn't know why she brought home every text book every night when she had no intention of studying.

"Every time you meditate, you have the opportunity to meet your Spirit Guides, but most people don't know this." Ashley began as she spoke softly, as though letting Chloe in on an ancient secret. "What you have to do is create a stable place between your conscious and unconscious mind to welcome them in. It's a place that you create within yourself, a place that you have envisioned in your own imagination; a place that makes you happy. Once you've done this, you will be able to retreat into it whenever you want." Ashley explained, using her right arm to emphasize her words while still hugging the formerly unloved puppy.

Chloe nodded as she listened, and she thought about where her place would be, but nothing came to mind.

"Where yours?" she asked.

"Mine's a beach. It's just a mile-long stretch of white sand next to an ocean with clear crystal blue waters. There are a few palm trees overhead, and giant shells on the ground."

"Beautiful." Chloe replied, imagining the calming blue waters her sister described.

"Okay, so once you create the place in your mind, you need to travel there in your meditation. Close your eyes, and go there."

"But, how do I do that?" Chloe asked, remembering her meditations. They seemed to resemble just a swirl of black mass. True, at times she would see colors, and even sometimes images would flash through her mind, but she had never actually tried to influence her visions.

"It's easy to do when you image the finer details of the place. Like, when I think of the beach, I see the grains of sand under my feet. I touch it, and feel pieces sprinkle through my fingers." Ashley replied, and she closed her eyes lightly as though she was right there on that beach again. "Notice the way you feel when you are in this special place - you should feel calm and relaxed."

The energy around Ashley seemed to calm down peacefully as she explained her secret place, and even the puppy dog in her arms had fallen asleep and was snoring ever so lightly. Ashley smiled at the puppy - it was confirmation that her cuddles and healing visions were working.

"As you get more comfortable in your sacred space, your Guides will come and visit you. They will be in different shapes and sizes and maybe not as you expected. Just be open to them and to what they have to say."

"Okay." Chloe nodded in agreement, taking the information in although she was still feeling slightly annoyed at her sister for not sharing this technique sooner. She had been suffering silently for months as the end of year twelve was creeping closer and closer and yet it was only now that her sister was sharing this insight with her!

"And so what did you do in this Spirit Guide world?"

"Hmm . . . I'd just ask them questions." Ashley said, shrugging her shoulders. Chloe could sense that her sister wasn't too eager to delve into her experiences, and understandably so, if it was to help deal with her heartbreak over the relationship with Brent. During those cold 8 months Ashley confided in no one, not even Chloe.

"And what did they tell you?"

"Well, at the time I was having difficulty accepting my reality, and they just reassured me that everything was as it should be."

"That doesn't really sound like much help though." Chloe rebutted, acting slightly unimpressed. If she picked up any self-help book she was sure she could've read that same line.

But she knew it wasn't enough to just read something and be changed, you had to live it. Ashley needed to let time heal her heartbreak, and she was a living example of someone mending her own heart. But where was the guideline for Chloe to follow? She couldn't find any book that gave her the advice that she needed.

"Well, maybe to you it doesn't," Ashley said. "But when you're in that space you feel connected to your authentic self. It's nice to be reassured with your own voice for once instead of someone else's, you know what I mean?"

No, Chloe didn't know. She felt as though she had only just gotten used to being a teenager and now everything was about to change all over again. Her adolescence was spent listening to her parents or her peers. She didn't really think for herself other than schoolwork or deciding what to do on the weekend. And here was Ashley telling her that she needed to reconnect with herself more than just through her meditation. She had no idea this was even possible!

"So what has this taught you?"

"Well, for one, it gave me the space to heal and see that my life really is truly amazing. I love my job and my friends, and being single and not in a relationship has allowed me to understand myself so much more! It was dangerous going straight from high school into adulthood with the same boyfriend. I didn't have time to understand myself well enough to transition from a teenage girl into a woman." Ashley replied smiling. She felt like she had finally solved the problem of her loneliness. "And Chloe, these are the last years of your teenage life! Will you enjoy them please? Before you hit your 20's and get old like me?"

"Yeah you're right." Chloe smiled, even though she felt that perhaps her life was too much fun and she needed to start being more serious about her future.

"Of course I'm right!" Ashley said as she winked. "Now speaking of fun, do you want to come to the party tonight?"

Chloe picked up her school bag and put it over her shoulder as she thought about the question. She wanted to go really badly, but her parents had organized a 9AM breakfast meeting with her to discuss her future. She had to come up with three options by that time.

"I have the breakfast with mum and dad, remember?" Chloe replied as she rolled her eyes. She didn't think her parents ever had to schedule such a meeting with Ashley, 'the angel child'.

"Ahh, how could I forget!" Ashley said as she laughed mockingly at Chloe. She had spoken to their parents about the talk and she knew it wasn't going to be too stressful, but just something to help push Chloe along. Her indecision was starting to bother everyone in the house, and this intervention was a proposed solution by her mother. "Okay, just go home and find these answers so you can stop stressing, your skin is starting to flare up."

Chloe peered over Ashley's shoulder into the mirror behind her. She was right, her cheeks were flushed red as though she was overheating. It was strange the way her body would react to situations before Chloe even realized she was so stressed.

"Go home, have a nice long bath and meditate." Ashley said as she closed the door.

Chloe agreed and left her sister to walk home. She paused in the front garden, hoping something would speak to her and give her the answers that she needed. Her eyes quivered as she looked up to the sky. The sun was setting, and the clouds hung low. They felt as gloomy as the emotion inside of her chest. She wanted to look at the sun to provide positive inspiration but something was stopping her, and she was unable to let the light in. The trees above her stood still. There was no breeze, no movement . . . just her, alone in the garden, looking up and begging to the skies for answers, talking to the universe, wanting to see clearly, wanting a hope, an idea, a thought to take ahold of her and become her possession.

A grasshopper jumped onto her leg, causing a shock of excitement throughout her body. Once she calmed again, she saw the creature was harmless. It was tiny and brown with long stick legs, and a body with a boxy-like frame as though it was made by origami.

"You're far from home," she said kindly, staring just long enough before it leapt away.

And she thought about the grasshopper's life, how it jumped from place to place, unsure where it was going to land, but confident that a landing place would exist. How she wished she could look at life like that of the grasshopper! Taking leaps of faith, following the sun, and being so playful. She worried too much. She knew that was her problem, that and being incredibly overly analytical. It was stressful to be this way, and she could see that her friends and family were starting to get irritated with her indecisiveness. Her greatest problem used to be overanalyzing something as simple as a text message from a new crush. But now the thoughts of deciding on a career had overtaken all others, and the scales were swaying from side to side as the steps to adulthood moved closer and closer, day by day.

Two

The Meeting Place

"Mum… Dad..?" Chloe called through the empty walls of the house. But no one was home.

Everyone is out having a good time but me! She scowled as she looked at herself in the hallway mirror and mimicked the funny looking girl who stared back at her. And here, as she looked at her reflection, she sympathized with the victimizing story she had created for herself. She had believed that she couldn't change her mind even if she wanted to.

Below the mirror was a bench on which rested a handwritten note with her name on it. It was written on her mum's favorite paper, and Chloe could feel the excitement her mum would have held as she wrote on it.

"Hi Darling,

Dad and I have gone out to dinner at the Grafton's, we will be home around 11.

Dinner's in the oven, and I bought you some of your favorite chocolate, shh, hide it from dad or he will eat it all!

Love you! Mom. xox

P.S. It's dad, I'm coming for the chocolate when I get home.

Chloe giggled to herself. Her parents acted like teenagers sometimes, but it made her smile seeing how in love they were. Everyone could see it. The neighbors envied their relationship, the way they always stood so strong through the thick and thin. Her mind would often flicker to the year of her thirteenth birthday when they were fighting all the time. It was the worst memory she ever had and for some reason her mind liked to play the same trick on her, by continuing to bring up this deeply saddened chapter of her life.

Her father had taken a job that paid well but he hated it, and slowly but surely, bit by bit, day by day, it destroyed their relationship because it went against everything her mother believed in. Her mother never cared for the money, what she wanted was happiness, she wanted to experience life and love. But it was an experience, her father would remind them. It was just a different experience, and he used to say, that 'there was no happiness that never saw pain'. And slowly by surely they stuck it out for a few years, earned the pretty pay check, and as soon as they paid off the house he left the company, but at what cost? Their marriage was on thin ice for those three years. Her father was overworked and exhausted from the moment he left the house to the time he came back, and the kids saw him for all of two hours and those two hours were spent trying to make mum happy because she could feel his exhaustion. And at the end of the day - she didn't want the money. But now, well . . . They sacrificed three years of their lives and it did make a big difference in the long run.

Now there was no debt, the children lived comfortably, and it was only three short years of their long life together, and they got through it. But the memory of those years stuck with Chloe, and still managed to pierce a nerve anytime the thought of them crossed her mind. She could still feel the pain that she witnessed coming from her parents, and it engraved in her a strong lesson: do not do anything that does not serve your happiness. She couldn't see clearly while she was still absorbed within the emotions stirred up by this memory, but it was all those little experiences around her, that added up to the main reason as to why she couldn't choose her life's path now.

"Do I tough it out for a few years to get materialistic things?" Chloe asked herself. "Swallow my dreams down low into the pit of my stomach and forget about what I want to do, so that I may attain short lived value in my day-to-day life. Or can I dive head first toward my passion? Stand at the edge of the cliffs above the terrifying rocks beneath and jump free, open my arms and allow the universe to guide me. Take the chance of the wind lifting me high or swallowing me whole to get where I feel I need to be. And even if I fell down, right down low, it was still an experience at the end of the day. Yes, it might not have been a pleasant one, but it was an experience, and those times of hardness and sadness and despair and hopelessness would soon build up the strength and courage I'd need to save myself." She knew she had the ability to do it - she just had to want to do it.

Chloe passed on the dinner in the oven, she didn't feel like it. She couldn't eat when she was stressed, she needed to know the answers to her questions. As her older sister had advised, she needed to delve deep inside of herself to search for them. It seemed to be the one part of her that couldn't let her down. It appeared to be the easy option and yet it terrified her the most, but what was she so afraid of? To find out the truth? I almost feel safer not knowing, she thought. She had begun to like the miserable side - at least it defined who she was. It made sense to her now that she had identified herself more with the misery than with anything else. It had been so long that she didn't know the alternative. But I don't want to feel this way anymore.

And so her meditation began. She settled in her bedroom, closed her eyes and took a deep breath in. With every breath out she threw all the troubles and worries and anxious feelings that she had bottled up inside and when she inhaled she swallowed confidence, pride, self-love and self-worth. She let the air swim around her body and as she did so, she envisioned little droplets of oxygen seeping into her bloodstream as it gracefully moved through her veins. And speaking words of positive optimism, she could sense her body feeling loved and nurtured. And as the air shifted around her body, filling with the positive energy, she let go of any fear or trauma that it had been holding onto.

"Let go! You do not belong within me." she said as the air flew out forcefully from her mouth in a great noisy exhale as though she were blowing a candle out from afar. And in her deep inhale she could feel her mind expand open and the gates of her heart beaming with pride, as though soaking in the light from above.

The air not only filled her lungs, she could also feel it entering into her auric field. It covered the outside of her in a giant bubble of love and light, protecting her. As the air swiftly moved inside her body it tore down any blockages that stood in its way. She was redefining her memory, clearing out anything that she didn't need anymore, and allowing the right messages, the right answers and the right questions to come her way. No longer did she identify herself with that miserable child who needed an answer. In that exact moment, in that exact memory of what she was creating, she felt at peace.

Her breath slowed down to a long drawn out pace. It was immensely relaxing, exuding the same feeling as though she was floating in a pool of water. But she felt as though her breath took an identity of its own. She felt as though it was no longer supporting her body, but her breath was now the life force that was creating everything around it. And as the realization of such an idea came into existence, she felt her body vibrate side to side. It shifted in quivers, a destructive process in contrast to the gentle breathing she was creating. It was as though her soul was shaking her body off and leaving it. She was wriggling from the shell of her existence, the same way a caterpillar would spring forth from a cocoon, and like a butterfly she flew. In her mind she soared through bright colors and oceans of patterns that evolved as fractals, entwining from the start of the time and exploring the journey and then coming back to the beginning.

Her mind cleared, and as it did, her eyes disappeared, and the sights that she saw were instead felt. She could feel the colors that travelled towards her as an auric field of energy, moving fast as it catapulted through her reality. Some pieces danced in slow vibrations, while others created a mark in the darkness, an open shell of light that stood strong, creating a whirlpool of matter to dive deep into and get lost in. How badly she wished she could fly into that hole and see what was on the other side! It was the closest she had ever felt to the entire universe.

After several minutes of deep breathing, the black matter began to settle. She knew that now would be the time for her to envision a sacred place. A place where she could feel calm and settled. But she didn't actually imagine it, instead, a place came forth to her. She was now standing on a long road that led over a hill. She couldn't see what was over that hill, but it didn't matter, because she somehow knew the road never ended, and she was content with where she was.

"This is the meeting place," she heard a voice inside her head.

She looked around, and saw that next to the road where she stood there was a large tree, with swinging branches that were aching to be swung. Tall grass grew either side of the pebble stone road. The sky was a clear blue, the pebble stone road was orange and the tall grass was bright green. The colors contrasted brilliantly with one another and the sun gleamed down on her with warmth. She didn't want to leave and stood still for several minutes. When she was ready, she jumped up to the branches of the tree to swing on. They swayed as her weight landed heavily onto them, and the sounds of their leaves rustled in the sun, creating a soft, purring sound. She jumped back down to the path and stood on one side of it, stirring the pebbles there with her feet. Each pebble was strategically placed amongst the earthly grass, leading her to wonder what the pebbles looked like from a birds eye view. Would they have created a pattern? The distance between each pebble seemed to have a message to say. She picked up one of the stones and saw that it was carved with a crystalized edge on one end, and yet soft and smooth on the opposite one. How that stone seemed to resemble her life before she went to high school! At first it was smooth sailing, easy going with no worries or cares, and then the rough edge, full of dips and shakes and cliffs to climb. It looked as if her life was filled with endless obstacles, but at the end it would always go smoothly, and the joyride would take charge, a pleasure slide of happiness. I wonder if my childhood had of been troubled, she thought, and the rough edge resembled me now. Would I have only joy and freedom to look forward to? And for a moment she wondered which life would have been better. She felt at peace with both.

She threw the pebble to the ground and watched as it skimmed as though flying through water. It bounced with little jumps, finding its new place to settle. How long must I wait here? she thought.

"This is the meeting place." she heard a voice inside of her say again. "They will be here soon."

She picked up a dandelion flower that had appeared in the grass next to the tree and blew the petals out to drift through the air. All the while the words echoed in her mind and she kept thinking, this is the meeting place.

First, a rustling of leaves in the tree startled her, then the vision of a jolly fat man hanging from the branches became visible to her next. His shirt was wrapped around like a Japanese kimono and a knot of hair was tied on the tip of his head. He reminded Chloe of a sumo wrestler. The image of him fluttered in and out quickly, as though he was testing her to see if it was safe for him to stay.

"Hello," Chloe said.

The chubby man jumped down next to Chloe, but he said nothing. He had a great big belly, large white teeth and a pointy mustache. Yet despite his huge blob of a body, he did not feel dangerous in the least. He merely resembled a fictional character, one of whom she had remembered seeing as a child on a cartoon. The two stared at each other for awhile. No words were uttered, yet a strange, overwhelming feeling of comfortable silence pervaded the distance between the them.

"Are you my spirit guide?" Chloe mentally asked.

"Yes." she heard his reply in her mind.

The man nodded, smiling with a deep, joyous gleam in his eyes, as a calm energy radiated through his vibration. Again, no words were spoken, but they did not need to be. Their words traveled through an electrical vibration that connected them together. It was the red string of time, never ending, forever long.

"Will you help me?" She pleaded desperately, feeling the weight of stress, anguish and disbelief as though it were an armor on her neck and shoulders. It was a great burden she had carried for too many years, the burden of not knowing the answer to her questions. The burden of desperately needing answers, but terrified of who to trust with giving them to her, unaware that the person she was seeking could very well be herself.

His reply of "Yes" cooed through his essence, as he bowed his head with grace, and blinked his eyes in harmony. He was showing her the greatest gift, the gift of patience.

"I am struggling to find the answers." she murmured quietly to herself.

"I am here to guide you." she heard his voice inside again, but no words came through his lips. She was reading his energy, and together they communicated with no words spoken. It was in the silence of her thoughts that the answers came through.

"Have you been with me all along?" Chloe asked, sensing a strange familiarity of his presence.

His outer appearance, the layers of skin and flesh, bore an unusual vision for her. She had never seen anything like it in real life. Chloe had never been to Asia, and had barely ever watched sumo wrestlers on television, but his plumpness emanated the cosy feeling of soothing cuddles. She desired to hold him, to feel the plumpness of his skin and jiggly jelly belly, for the attraction of the unusual was calling to her, and as she thought about what it would be like to hug him, she felt she was doing so. He stood far away from her, but she felt the same relief through the mental stimulation as though it were physically happening. She felt the emotional release that was achieved by two hearts crossing over one another, and as she did so, she trusted her guide, and began to breathe a little easier, and the cage she had built that burdened her shoulders, didn't feel as heavy anymore.

"What's your name?" she asked, now accepting his place by her side.

"It's not my name, but you can call me Sam." he said, with a deep voice.

Chloe smiled, and she laughed to herself as a memory from her childhood raced through her mind. It was the strong memory of an imaginary friend who she named Sam. This imaginary friend was a lion, and he would appear at times of difficulty, when she needed strength and courage to get through the day. He came back to visit her in her dreams when her parents were fighting, oddly enough. They would stream through the jungle together, she on the lions' back, holding tightly to his mane, and watching other animals go by. All at peace; there was nothing to be feared.

She looked to Sam and smiled.

"You've been with me my whole life haven't you?"

He returned the smile with a sense of proudness like a father figure and slowly nodded his head. It was true. Whether in her dreams, or the sense of something near her, she could always feel his presence. His energy was unmistakable.

She stood and stared a little longer at him, relishing the peaceful nature of existence she felt from their connection. On the land where they stood, she could feel the air breeze slowly in the space that lay between them. It connected their energies into a single energy, that bounced far outside of her visual range, and she felt him through the layers she had built around her heart.

The sun shone strongly upon them, blanketing the land with loving warmth. There was no land untouched, no area left deprived, and for several seconds Chloe allowed herself to be completely absorbed in the heat from the sun. It crisped her body with a heavenly glow, giving life to the trees and nature around her. She looked back to Sam and smiled, but now standing next to him was her own shadow, dark, depressed and staring back at her.

She looked to Sam and back to her shadow. Its face resembled that of hers, but with its teeth clenched in bitterness, and eyes that squinted with sadness, red, and raw, from endless tears. Sam looked to the shadow and back to Chloe.

"What do you see?" he asked, searching the space for what Chloe was looking at.

"I see sadness, emptiness and misery. Fear, and loneliness . . ." the words dribbled from Chloe's mouth. She felt and alarming attachment to them, as though they were the words that helped to define herself, and yet she prayed that it wasn't true.

"This is your shadow. This is what is preventing you from moving forward right now." Sam said as he pointed to the cutout version of Chloe.

"How do I fix it? By thinking positively?" Chloe asked, this was the only answer she thought that could remove the negative thoughts from her mind.

"No, there is more to it than that." Same replied, holding his hand out to the shadow.

"There is?"

"We need to feel this shadow first, completely. Let's see what it has to say. Only through the shadow can we get to the light. The answer you seek is through this shadow, not around it."

Chloe looked to the shadow, it appeared as though it weighed heavy on the ground. It was sticky on the path like a big mess of muddy tar, wanting anything that came near it to stick to it.

"Are you willing to explore this shadow with me? Observe the depth of this shadow and all that it can possibly contain? We will move through it like water, floating in the current, washing over rocks and through valleys."

"Will you help explore this shadow with me?" she asked.

"If you wish." he replied. But the reply came from within herself, echoing in her heart, and her mind.

Sam looked to the left where a circular vortex was beginning to swirl. It swirled every so slowly to begin with, and became a captivating reflection of Chloe's world upside down. It continued to evolve, changing with every moment that existed, turning itself into something different to what it was before. The longer Chloe stared, the more it changed, the more it closed in and reopened on itself. Now, the spinning had moved into a giant fortress of black matter, with twinkling stars enveloping the edges of the opening. She looked to Sam, whose face held no expression. The pointy whiskers on his beard lifted slightly higher, as though magnified from the opening of energy.

"Shall we face this shadow?" he asked, holding his hand out to her, and then bringing it closer to the circle, presenting her with the opportunity to go through.

Chloe looked around the land once more before surrendering to the change. The sun above shone greatly on their heads, and she closed her eyes and took a deep breath. Behind her closed eyes she saw the same vibrations of black circles and colored lines she had seen with her eyes open. They resembled that of the vortex circle that Sam had presented to her. She thought she would feel fear but she did not - there was no emotion in this vision. Then she opened her eyes and looked at Sam.

"I am ready." she said.

Holding hands, they walked through the vortex, and a burning sensation tickled over her body, the feeling she would have imagined when walking through a fire. But the safety of Sam's hand guiding her gave her comfort, and the burning sensation turned to chills, as though her whole body was vibrating with a great awakening. For the first time in many years, she felt completely alive.

They stepped through the circle, but when the twirling came to a stop, Chloe found herself standing on the same spot as before. It was exactly the same, with the sun in the same position, the tree above their heads, and the same tall grass on the sides of the path.

"I don't understand." Chloe said as she looked around the world as it appeared once before.

But Sam wouldn't talk to her; he wouldn't even move. He wouldn't budge, and he was no longer holding her hand. He turned as though he was a statue, a mere shadow of himself. Chloe looked to the ground, seeing the reflection of her own shadow clearly, standing strong right next to her.

Curious, she walked closer to it, and examined the great darkness that was attached to her light and she stood within it. It resembled a layer of murky glass, but when looking through the glass she felt an overwhelming emotion of fear, hate, regret and sadness. And as she looked to the world through her shadow, it was no longer as she remembered, rather a deep sadness that had overtaken every aspect of where she looked. The grass was dead. It was still tall having not been cut, but it hung heavily on the ground, and the sun was nowhere to be seen. It was cold, it was dark, and it felt evil. The tree had insects and bugs eating its flesh, like a tortured animal, being sucked dry from everything that came from it. The leaves were gone, it bore no fruit, and the branches were skinned, rotted from the inside out.

"What is this madness you have taken me to?" Chloe asked Sam. She tried to walk away from the shadow, but it kept following her gaze, jumping in front of her, and she found herself unable to move it, to see the beautiful nature that once lay before her.

She kept staring at the shadow - stared at it until her vision became blurred, and in between the blurred spaces she could see herself, holding happiness and sadness in opposite hands.

"What am I seeking from this?" she asked her shadow, as the emotions clouded her mind. The sadness weighed heavily on the scales, almost three times the size of her happiness. As she examined each weight, she felt them both completely, observing and honoring their existence. She knew it was not possible for happiness to overtake sadness all of the time, but it was the top-heaviness of sadness that tipped Chloe off track too often, unbalancing her Soul and triggering a victimizing cry. Too often she would feel the depth of depression alive in her mind, instead of observing it and letting it go for what it was. And she realized in that moment of looking at her emotions that she was the one who kept her scales unbalanced. It was unbalanced because she was continuously choosing to feed sadness instead of happiness, keeping herself in misery.

"I acknowledge your existence and I accept you as a part of me. But I chose balance, and I release you from me." she said as she blew into the dark space and mentally balanced the scales before her. The shadow remained dark, but the emotional feeling that weighed heavily upon it became lighter, softer, and pleasurable to touch. And then the shadow stood behind her, not in front of her. She knew it would never leave her, and that was okay. She was ready to face it head on, and accept that this darkness was a part of her, herself.

"Sam, come back to me." she pleaded. "I still need your guidance, I need to know what to do with my life. I have to make decisions now."

They were interrupted as an ancient turtle slowly walked up the pathway, its small head protruding through the beautiful, antique shell that weighed heavy on its back. The turtle walked ever so slowly and with such pride. Carrying his home wherever he went, he did not waiver but walked through the pathway. The shell molded into a part of his existence, and when staring at it closely it appeared heavy, but when looking at the big picture, it just was. It was a trophy of beauty, a magnetic display of uniqueness. The layers of its skin radiated strength, wisdom and knowledge. And even though the turtle walked at a slow pace, it did not care who or what was around, and did not notice either Chloe or Sam. He just carried on his business, sticking to himself and knowing that the path before him was laid out for him.

Sam smiled and nodded at the turtle, and then at Chloe. She could feel his voice soothe through to her.

"Go slow and enjoy." Chloe heard in her mind.

The soft sound of bells chimed through the space where she stood with Sam. It echoed throughout the land, making a pitter patter sound as gentle as rain. Even so, the sound disrupted the calmness in the space and cluttered her mind, rendering her unable to focus. Sam half smiled, the right side of his lip reaching up to his cheek, as though happy to have met Chloe but knowing the time had come for her to leave. She ran closer to him and hugged him, feeling the squishiness of his skin, the comfort of his chubby belly.

"I love you." she said.

"I love you." he said.

"It's time for me to go, isn't it?"

He nodded.

She didn't want to. She felt so safe in his presence. No one was around them, no one was disturbing them, and no thoughts were entering her mind other than focusing on the two of them together, sharing words and laughter and creating memories.

"Can I come back to you?" she asked.

"I will always be here, right here." he said, "Available whenever you need me."

"But what if I can't find you?"

"Then your mind is not quiet enough."

Suddenly, Chloe opened her eyes to the sound of her mum and father giggling. They had come home from the party. Her father was making jokes and her mother was laughing historically in short breaths.

"Rob, Rob . . . Shh . . . Chloe might be asleep."

Chloe smiled. She loved hearing them talk about her like a little baby needing her rest, and although she had grown up and was almost an adult, she loved the family nest that still resided within the home.

"It's okay, I'm awake." Chloe yelled through the door as she stood up and walked through to greet them. "How was the party?"

"Oh, your father wouldn't stop dancing."

"Twinkle toes they used to call me!" Her father nodded proudly as he mimicked a moon walk across the hardwood floors.

"Oh honey, I still call you twinkle toes." Her mother smiled cheekily, giving him the same love and affection that she did over twenty years ago.

And Chloe could see that was the secret. The strength behind their relationship was from the little things. Their admiration for each other blazed in strength as the years went on and their respect was mutual. Their love was an evolving flower that blossomed more beautifully as time passed and together they chose to tackle every obstacle with grace and patience.

"What's been happening? Where's Ashley?" her father asked as he sat down and took off his shoes in the hallway. The ribbon laces in his brown shoes were Chloe's favorite, and she loved the sense of style her father had. He dismissed everyone else's opinion and went with what felt good.

"Ashley's gone to a concert sweetheart." her mother called from the kitchen as she poured three glasses of water.

"And you didn't want to go?" her father asked Chloe surprised.

"No, I've got too much on my mind with our meeting and all." she half smiled in reply and raised her eyebrows.

"Go on, tell me what's going on." Her father stopped what he was doing and patted the chair next to him, prompting her to join him. But she stood strong against the wall, not yet ready to admit complete defeat.

"I just, I don't know what to do when high school finishes. I have no direction. I have absolutely no clue whatsoever."

"Chloe that's okay, your mother and I just want you to have a few options tomorrow. They don't have to be definite, just something."

Chloe looked up at him sheepishly, like a little child being told what to do.

"None of us have the answers to this, you realize that?" he said. "There is no wrong or right choice, there are just different paths, different ways of life. And if one doesn't work then you jump to another, there's nothing wrong with that. There's nothing bad about it - it just is. Okay?"

"Okay." Chloe replied as her mother handed her a glass of water.

"What do you think you want to do?" her mother asked, now joining her father on the sofa.

"Well, I want to paint. It's the only thing in my mind that I want to do. It's what I like doing the most." Chloe recited, realizing that painting had always been her passion. But the thought of trying to make a living off a hobby felt too daunting.

"So paint." Her father and mother nodded together.

"But . . . How? I don't have the confidence."

"Chloe, anything you create is incredible, you know that. How can we help you gain the confidence?" her father asked, squinting his eyes slightly, prompting a response.

"I don't know… Maybe I need to study more?" But Chloe didn't really believe that study would be the answer. After having almost completed 12 years of school, the thought of continuing with more didn't sound very fun. But this was where she choked up, she just didn't know how to support her artistic dream.

"So then study. Chloe, whatever you want to do, your mother and I will support you, you know this."

Chloe nodded.

"First thing tomorrow, the assignment at our breakfast meeting will be to look up the best art school for you to attend, whether it's a full time university or a part time college, okay?"

Chloe smiled and hugged her father tightly. And then she kissed her mother on the cheek goodnight, and fell into a deep sleep.

Three

Soul Connections

Chloe woke up early with a strange feeling in her chest. It felt like while she was sleeping her ribs had been crushed. She had difficulty breathing, and without warning a slow wheezing sound emanated from her mouth. She sat upright, and took a big drink of water from the glass that was sitting on her bedside table. But the water didn't clear and refresh her mind as she expected. Usually, a drink of clean water would clear her throat, but this time it didn't. Instead, a sad feeling rushed through her body, and a feeling of rattled displacement, echoed in her mind. Something didn't feel right.

"Mom . . . Dad . . ."

She jumped up and went to their bedroom door, but it was shut tight. Next she tried her sister Ashley's door, but it too was closed. Her whole family was still asleep and everything appeared to be normal - after all it was only 6am.

The entry to the kitchen was calling her name, and she walked through the natural sunlight seeping into the room, yearning to make a cup of coffee. She stood on the tip of her toes, feeling the base of her feet stretch out onto the cool tiles, providing a stable balance of support beneath. As she poured the coffee grains she stretched up high, feeling her body extend in ways that it hadn't moved for at least a day. It was deeply nourishing.

She enjoyed moving and stretching in extremes as she gathered the things she needed for her morning ritual. As she made her breakfast, she designed it as a masterpiece. She watched the grains of coffee roll over each other as they landed inside the Italian espresso maker. The fire from the stove clicked noisily, and as she looked at it, she marveled at the sight of such beauty: how quickly the flames licked around the edges of the coffeepot, and the stirring of the water as it escaped the heat below. She leaned on her elbows and moved as closely as she could to the fire to listen to the popping sound of the water as it evaporated up through the tunnel into the safety above. She liked to imagine that the water was dancing above the flames. It flirted and played in their presence, moving quickly with shuddering with breaths. Or sometimes perhaps the water needed to escape, and it was jumping high, wanting to detach itself from its current situation. And slowly, over the flames the water would escape, whether it was to rest from too much dancing, or from a need to escape from the dramatic heat. Little by little the steam evaporated up into the top of the espresso maker, oozing a delicious scent of fresh ground coffee, tickling the tastebuds of whoever was nearby. Chloe poured the hot coffee into her favorite cup. It was painted with Japanese artwork on its edge and had no handle. Sometimes it was too hot to carry, but she liked the discipline of needing to be cautious with everything she did - just like the Japanese did, taking pride in their every movement. And with coffee in one hand, and an apple in the other, she nestled by the window to read a chapter of her favorite book. But the birds outside weren't singing their usual song, and the feeling of something not right still tapped on the inside of her mind.

The landline phone rang louder than usual. How could that be? Chloe wondered. Her father picked it up from his bedroom and she could hear him speaking in a mumbled voice. Then she heard her mother crying. Then the branches of a tree near her house began banging against the window, and the dogs next door were barking loudly. And she could still hear her mother crying, and the words from her father telling her with a stern voice, that everything's going to be alright.

The air around Chloe felt thinner than usual, and it started to hurt to breathe again. She could feel tears welling deeply within her eyes before her father even opened the door, pouring heavily onto her face. They were compiled of a mixture of terror and fear. Her skin became hot. Then her father, dressed to go out, exited his bedroom with a look on his face that Chloe knew she would never forget.

"There's been an accident." he said.

Chloe didn't need to know anymore. She ran to her sisters' room, and opened the door. The bed was made. Not slept in. She never came home last night.

"Where is she?" Chloe asked, as her mother walked out of the bedroom dressed and ready to leave.

"She's in the hospital, quick, get dressed." her father instructed, as he walked briskly toward Chloe to hug her.

"And?"

"There was a car accident early this morning." her father said. "The other car was a drunk driver, it wasn't her fault." he added in softly under his breath.

"Is she okay?" The tears from Chloe's eyes poured down too quickly over her face and they fell to the floor before she could catch them.

"Her ribs are broken and she has some internal organ damage. She's having difficulty breathing but her heart is beating strong, and all her injuries will heal." her father explained. But Chloe felt frozen, she couldn't move, she just wanted to cry. "She's been in and out of consciousness. Chloe, she's going to look worse than how she feels, okay?"

Chloe nodded as her mother hugged Chloe too and then walked her back into her bedroom to get dressed.

"We need you to be brave for us. For Ashley. She needs your support." she said, pulling out some jeans and a jumper for Chloe to wear.

No one spoke while they drove to the hospital. Chloe's mum was quietly sobbing to herself, and her father was holding her mother's hand tightly.

"It's going to be okay everyone, you know?" he said as looked at Chloe in the review mirror.

Chloe's eyes were red from tears but she had cried a lot and knew that she needed to be strong for her mother, like her father was. Plus, it still hurt her to breathe and she had a hard time crying when she was in so much pain.

The three of them walked through the white corridors of the hospital, feeling the stale energy compressed in the space like vacant souls crossing over. The people around them who were visiting loved ones appeared so struck with grief that they were like zombies, walking side by side and searching for something to hold onto.

Ashley lay in a coma-like state with a blackened and bruised face. There were cords coming out of everywhere, and the heart monitor's beeping sound vibrated through the room far too loudly. Their mom took Ashley's forearm and tickled her skin, combing over her light freckles while doing so and kissing her forehead gently.

"Thank you for coming in so quickly." the Indian doctor said, as he walked into the room to explain what had happened. "I'm Dr. Clive, and I've been looking after Ashley." He smiled with sincerity as he looked over his clipboard and explained Ashley's injuries. "Although she has not regained conscious, she's showing some form of awareness and that's a good sign. But we won't know if there will be any permanent damage until she wakes up."

"Can I talk to you for a minute?" their father asked as he walked Dr. Clive outside. Chloe could tell there was more that needed to be said but her father didn't want the women to be more worried than necessary.

Chloe and her mum held hands as they both touched Ashley. There was a line of loving energy that moved through and among the three of them, and Chloe could feel it was moving strong, feeding love and support into Ashley's body and providing her with new tools to fight with. Her face looked so peaceful. So gentle and peaceful.

Their father walked back through the door, his face grim from the conversation with the doctor. No one asked him any questions. They knew he would've just wanted to know the worst and best case scenario, and exactly as he thought, the women preferred not to know until he knew what was happening for sure. They liked to think optimistically, to be able to believe that the best was going to happen.

The time passed slowly as they sat around Ashley's bed. They spoke little. Every now and again one of them would sit and talk to her asking where she was and when she was coming back. They told her often that they loved her and for her to please come back. A few times they pleaded by telling her that when she came back mom would make her favorite dessert or meal. Her father said she was allowed to borrow the car whenever she wanted, and her mother said she would bring her fresh flowers to her room every morning. Everyone was trying to plead, bargain and beg for Ashley to come back - whatever they could think of to help her come back to them.

Chloe and her mother and father, waited all afternoon for Ashley to regain consciousness. She murmured a few words here and there and was trying to come back. After some time a nurse came and told them that visiting hours were over and it was time to go home, get some food and rest.

They returned home and stumbled through the front door.

"What does everyone feel like eating?" Chloe's mom said, mechanically walking to the kitchen while trying to hold her emotions inside.

But no one was hungry. They all hugged each other tightly and said a prayer together, promising one another that they would get some sleep.

Chloe woke up wide awake at 5am and for a second she forgot everything that had happened - but it was only for the smallest fraction of a second. The energy of her sister was missing in the house, and Chloe could feel its absence. She remembered her sister in pain in the hospital. She remembered her own pathetic, wasted use of her own life and she felt very guilty for having no desire to better herself. There was just such a strange feeling of emptiness inside her. She had no motivation, no direction, no feeling of wanting to do anything. She felt a combination of boredom about how to pass the time, mixed with despair and misery. If she were to define one specific emotion she was feeling it was simply sadness for her sister's being injured and in a coma, and how badly she wished to trade places with her. She should've. It made sense. She felt completely exhausted even though she had just woken up. It was a mental and emotional exhaustion, not just physical. She had no desire to get out of bed. She couldn't face reality while her sister was lying unconscious.

She laid back down, and let herself drift back to sleep, thinking her reality was just a bad dream that she needed to sleep off. A few days passed by in a similar pattern: Visit her sister in the hospital, eat, sleep. Ashley would murmur and she began to wake up a little bit at times, but most of the time she was unconscious and needed more rest. School had ended and the summer vacation had began but Chloe didn't feel like celebrating. She was constantly worried. On the ninth day she finally had some energy when she got out of bed.

Chloe sat up and slumped her body on the edge of the bed, shoulders extended down and chin low to her chest. She stretched her neck out slightly and felt a release of tension.

Feeling that energy in her neck was the only way she could focus her mind on anything other than her sister's condition. Otherwise, her mind was just mush. No thoughts. No emotions. Her body was still drained from crying the day before. Take deep breaths, she kept telling herself. Look left, she heard a voice inside her mind say. She peeked to her side and stared at her paint box. It called to her. Chloe, come find me, she heard it say. She stood and did so, and picking up a pot of dark purple paint, squeezed it onto her palette, took her paintbrush, and began to paint.

Hours flew by in what seemed like seconds. Her shirt was covered in paint - she hadn't even bothered to change into her apron. And with a final touch of yellow, she exhaled with a great sigh of relief. She had finished. The emotion had been released, but, she was too terrified to look at what she had created. Her dance with the painting had overtaken her mind and body. It was as though she had blanked out for hours, twisting and turning her body in an emotional rush. And when she finally did look, she gasped! She saw an open wound splattered across the canvas. Full of raw emotion, it was a plea for help and a scream to make a deal with the devil for her to switch places with her sister. Ashley had everything going for her. She was far more beautiful than Chloe, smart, had her life on track and loved her job. And here was Chloe with no idea what she was doing, little confidence in how she was going to survive in the real world and a lack of enthusiasm for moving in any direction. But the emotion on the canvas spoke to her. In amongst the terror and madness that she had created, she felt a small window of glowing opportunity.

In a small sliver of blue paint, she had drawn a shape that reminded her of the turtle she saw with Sam, her Spirit Guide, and the turtle whispered to her to "Have faith". To stay grounded and not allow her emotions to completely override her rationality in daily life. Yes, she could tap into her emotions when creating a masterpiece, but that was the great beauty in it - she knew she could use her emotions to draw and create and paint and that this would release her nervous energy. But the turtle - she thought of how the turtle walked: close to the ground, slow, determined, and persistent. Her sister would get better over time, and she, herself would figure out her true calling in life. She drew in the lines of the turtles back, thinking about the ancient structure of the shell, how the cage that it built protected him, and what a burden he carried by holding that cage so close to his back. I wonder if he ever wishes to remove it? But then, she could also see how he felt safe in his home.

"Chloe.." her mother interrupted her, knocking on the door.

"Come in Mama." Chloe replied as she took off her paint-stained shirt and changed into something clean.

"Oh wow, Chloe, that's beautiful!" her mother said as she walked magnetically to the painting, as though it had pulled her quickly to it.

And in light of everything that had happened, Chloe just saw her mother looking so very beautiful. The afternoon sun was softly gazing through the window, and it glistened on her mother's face where she had been crying. Her skin, soft and dewed, her blonde hair curled around her jawline.

"Do you really like it Mama?" Chloe asked as she looked to her painting with confusion. She wasn't sure if she even liked it herself. To her it was just an overload of emotion thrown against a canvas, a mixture of fear and love confined in one small square of space.

"Yes my darling, I can feel so much love in this drawing. Do you remember making it?" she asked, knowing very well that throughout her whole childhood her daughter would have dizzy spells when she painted. It was an alarming message, her mother thought at first. When she interrupted her child before the painting was done, Chloe's expression was vacant, her eyes barely able to focus on her mother, and the words she spoke made little sense. Now, she understood that it was another entity taking over Chloe's body. But not in a bad way - in a good way. It was her soul communicating through her, Ashley would explain, being the one in the family who was most in touch with the spirit world. The Chloe they knew and loved always came back after these spells, and they began to realize there was a message to be learned from the painting she had created. Sometimes the painting would portray a stressful image, an image that wasn't necessarily reflective of Chloe but created for someone else. And this painting was for Ashley.

"No I don't remember making it, mom. I just know that I love you. You really understand me." she said as she hugged her mother tightly, nuzzling her head inside her shoulder. That comforting feeling of family, the bloodline of energy, was irreplaceable. She felt soothed by her mothers' touch. But at the same time as it was comforting, it enabled Chloe to release her tense thoughts, and just be completely herself.

And inside the walls of the home they had built, quietly, she wept into her mother's arms.

"We have to be strong for each other Chloe." her mother said as she patted her youngest daughter on the back. "Ashely's going to get better, you will see."

"But even if she does, we don't even know what kind of after effects she might have . . . What if she's brain damaged?" Chloe asked, crying even harder than before at the idea of what could be. It felt so real, and she scolded herself for imaging the worst.

"Don't think like that Chloe, that doesn't help anyone okay?" her mother said seriously as she lifted Chloe's chin and looked her straight in the eye.

Chloe nodded and then nuzzled her head tighter into her mother's chest. She cried again, angry at herself for thinking that way.

"I believe Ashley is still with us Chloe. She is having too much fun dancing in the galaxy and doesn't want to come back to Earth." her mother joked. They all knew Ashley's love for space, the planets and the supernatural. "We just need to keep praying and keep moving forward. Think what Ashley would want you to be doing, and do everything for her. Imagine she is here, pushing you along, okay?"

Chloe released her mothers' hug and smiled at her positivity. The wrinkles around her mother's eyes creased softly. The familiarity was comforting and Chloe felt at ease. There was so much strength in her mother's presence.

"Why don't you go visit some art schools with your father? It will help distract both your minds."

"But I feel guilty doing that when Ashley is lying unconscious in a hospital bed."

"No, it's what she would've wanted. And then when you get accepted, you can tell her all about it, and maybe it will be a good reason for her to come back to us." her mum said and smiled.

Chloe agreed. She had a shower and met her father in the living room. He was already researching schools he thought would be appropriate. They settled on one together and Chloe felt excited! It was something for her to look forward to. As she submitted her application form online, the phone rang from the hospital. Ashley had regained consciousness.

Four

A Message From Above

Ashley was asleep when her family arrived. And the three sat quietly in the room waiting for her to wake up. No words were spoken, but the moment they sat down her eyes fluttered. She knew they were there. And after a long hour, which felt like five, she slowly, very slowly, opened her eyes.

"I'm . . . Sorry . . . To have worried you all. . ." She managed to speak in between soft breaths.

Her mother jumped up quickly, kissing her on the forehead.

"Shh.. my darling. There is nothing to be sorry about. You are okay, and we're all very happy that you are."

Her mother patted her daughters' hand, caressing the edges of her skin. Ashley nodded lightly, her eyes opening and closing in slow motion. The four sat in the room for awhile talking to Ashley, letting her listen to the sound of their voices.

After a few hours the doctor interrupted them.

"Hello everyone. How's she doing?" he asked, a cheery smile on his dark-skinned face. He was very handsome, with caring, loving eyes.

"Hello." Ashley spoke faintly as the doctor came and adjusted the bandages around her face.

"Hi Ashley," he said soothingly. "Do you remember what happened to you?"

Ashley closed her eyes and shook her head.

"No . . . maybe I . . . don't . . . want to . . . remember?" she replied in long draw out breaths.

"Probably." The Indian-looking doctor nodded. "The body goes into a state of shock after an accident like yours. It may take you months, even years, to remember. And of course you don't have to remember."

Ashley lightly nodded again and looked to her sister, half smiling. Chloe smiled back in reassurance, happy to connect with her sister once more.

"How long will she be in hospital for?" Chloe asked the doctor, sensing it was Ashley's unspoken question.

"It's hard to say. Ashley has broken both sides of her ribs and the top right of her collarbone. Her internal organs have been injured; we're still running some tests and will know more later how extensive they are. Fortunately, although her skull has been bruised, she has no brain damage, and the fact that she's been coming in and out of consciousness is a good sign." He smiled soothingly. "And everything appears to be working right at the moment - Ashley you must have some powerful angels looking over you."

"I'm so tired ..." she said as she nodded off lightly.

"You are welcome to stay as long as you like today of course, but just try not to ask her too many questions. She needs her rest."

"Okay, sure doctor. Whatever she needs." her father said as the three stood up and kissed Ashley goodbye.

"Wait, can I speak to Chloe?" Ashley whispered as they all started to leave.

"Of course sweetheart, we will wait outside."

Chloe sat on the edge of the bed, holding her sister's good hand.

Ashley opened her lips slightly. She wanted to be able to move more freely but was unable to.

"I had an out of body experience when I was unconscious Chloe." She smiled with a faraway look in her eyes. It was as though she knew where she was, and she didn't want to come back.

"What happened?" Chloe said as she moved closer to Ashley, sitting on the bed so that she wouldn't have to strain her voice too much.

"It was the most surreal experience I've ever had. I felt attached to my body by a long silver rope. I flew over mountains, and high above the sky. I played in the darkness between the stars and in the stardust. It was so beautiful Chloe." she said slowly as she closed her eyes again, reliving the memory. "But most importantly, I saw you. I saw you painting a beautiful blue lake with a great big turtle swimming in it. And everything became so clear." Ashley opened her eyes back up and looked at her sister as she tried to smile. "You are an artist Chloe. I want you to pursue your painting. I believe it is what you are meant to do. You need to do this. It's your career path."

Chloe felt tears of joy flood down her cheeks. Her sister was giving her a message from afar, and yet she felt very sad. She was devastated that through a serious auto accident, such a beautiful truth would be uncovered. And yet at the same time, she was relieved. She had received words of wisdom from above. It was miraculous!

"Ashley, I was painting that very picture! I painted it for you. There is a blue lake and a turtle swimming in it it! That's so weird."

"I'm not surprised. I'm telling you, I saw you. Part of the reason I wanted to get home was to tell you about how incredibly talented you are. I believe in you."

Chloe smiled with warm, fuzzy feelings shooting around her body, and her blood tickled at the surface of her skin, creating little bumps on it and a shiver in her spine. She was feeling as though a strange truth had been generated between them.

"I'll bring the painting in for you next time. See, the turtle is you, Ashley! It has begun its journey. It's a slow swim to recovery, but you will get there Ashley."

"I love it, thank you." Ashley replied, although her eye lids closed lightly again.

"You're so brave Ashley, you really are a true inspiration."

"It's just a new challenge in life, a step of transformation; it's been awhile since I've had one." She attempted another smile at Chloe, but all she could do was open her mouth just wide enough to expose her teeth.

"And then what happens?" Chloe asked, wondering what kind of transformation this could be. She couldn't believe how calm she was.

"Then I will claim my space here on this Earth and value my life in a different light. This must have happened for a greater cause, a big jump to shift my life elsewhere. I'm not sure where yet, but it will come."

Chloe looked at her sister admiringly. She clearly was the most optimistic person she had ever met, and she was proud to call her her sister.

"Now, what are we going to do about your painting? Have you given it much thought?"

"I'm applying to university. Mom and dad think it will help build my confidence. Well that's what they said the night before the . . ."

Chloe's words drifted, she didn't dare speak about what had happened, and instead felt guilty again that they hadn't switched places.

"Before the accident, Chloe. It's okay, we can talk about it. It happened." Ashley said as she filled in Chloe's words.

"Ashley I should've been with you." Chloe confessed, kneeling next to the bed and holding her sisters' hand.

"Why?" she asked, but it was more of a rhetorical question. "This is my lesson, Chloe."

As Ashley talked Chloe noticed that she had a different look in her eyes. It was a peculiar mixture of exhaustion, surrender, and pleasure. It was as though the experience had created a new awakening for her. She appeared as if she was drifting between two different worlds of consciousness. And even now, with Ashley lying on the hospital bed, seriously injured and unable to leave, Chloe still wished she had switched places with her . . . But not for the reasons she had originally felt. No, now she saw something in her sister that she aspired to have for herself. It was her sister's outlook of constant positivity, an understanding appreciation of an ultimate trust in the world around her, in her universe and her Guides. Yet Chloe felt that no matter how hard she tried, she would never be able to reach that same level of happiness, and it pained Chloe more than she cared to admit.

Five

Time For A Change

"Mrs. Salters will see you now." the sturdy looking receptionist said as she peered over her glasses at Chloe and pointed to a wooden door on the right.

Each step that Chloe took towards that door felt like an eternity. The door was only two feet away, but each step pushed her back another foot. She had built her dreams up behind that door. She prayed that her hard work would be recognized. That the lady would say - "You are everything we have been looking for." But she felt a tightness in her chest that made it difficult to breathe, and her throat was so dry she couldn't swallow.

Chloe opened the door to see a middle-aged lady with brown hair pulled back into a tight, low bun. Mrs. Salters smiled warmly, and suggested that Chloe take a seat across from the large wooden desk in front of her.

"Let's start with why you want to study at our school, shall we?" she asked, although Chloe couldn't help but feel as though she was seeking compliments to the school. Chloe had no problem giving them - she had done her research and she knew it was the best school for the direction she wished to pursue.

"I want to learn about the different styles in art and how I can incorporate them into my artwork. And most importantly

I want to challenge my thinking." Chloe said shyly as she opened her portfolio and placed it on the desk in front of Mrs. Salters, cringing as she did so. This blocked the energy that traveled through her body, making her shake with nerves, but she couldn't keep her feelings of insecurity from surfacing. She felt as though her artwork reflected that of a tormented child, an emotional disaster splattered across the canvases. She held her breath, silently awaiting Mrs. Salters critique.

"Your style is quite strong Chloe." Mrs. Salters commented as she turned each page, staring at each image for less than two seconds. "I don't necessarily think that it is a bad thing, but here, we encourage students to expand their mind, to open up new doors. It's a matter of streamlining your paintings so you will be able to sell them as pieces of artwork." She hesitated, her mouth slightly open and tongue to the roof of it, as though deep in thought. "I don't think you have much flexibility in your vision that would enable you to explore different pathways. I think you should just keep doing what you are doing, but perhaps attend a business school or something more along the lines of how to execute your paintings."

Chloe's mind rolled with confusion. What was this woman saying? Was this a rejection? Was she actually saying no, you are not invited to attend my school? Wasn't Chloe the one who would be paying them? Chloe nodded silently, but she wasn't listening anymore to what Mrs. Salters was saying. Her mouth was opening and closing and words were coming out, but they seemed irrelevant - her facial expressions said it all. Her eyes squinted with a sympathetic look, and her mouth curved upwards, a smile that was saying to her, "Sorry, but life goes on".

The next few minutes rolled past in a split second, and before she knew it, she was standing outside the university, holding her pride and joy in her hands and for the first time feeling disgusted with her work. All she wanted to do was throw it in the trashcan. She could feel the tears in her eyes that were flowing with sadness. A sense of hopelessness had completely struck her down. She felt useless and for the first time in her entire life she felt like she didn't want to be alive anymore. Her dreams of what she wanted to do were laughed at, her passion, torn apart and shredded by the world's best art school's professional opinion. Her world was crashing around her, one never ending madness swirling upwards into a tornado. And when it stopped spinning, a hurricane had flooded through, diminishing everything that she touched, wiping the slate clean and forcing her to start all over again.

She walked to the bus stop to go home, dragging her feet behind and trying to wipe the tears away. Oh why did I forget to take my sunglasses today? She got angry at herself. The one day I have to hide my face and I forget my sunglasses. She cursed herself again.

Chloe arrived to the bus stop milliseconds after the bus left. Just my luck. she sighed, stomping her feet with anger and kicking the side of the bench at the bus stop. Her tears had finally stopped now, and she felt angry. Angry at life for making her feel this way. Angry at the world for being so cruel. She felt confined within a vortex of emotions, swirling helplessly around and around, with nothing to grab onto. Nothing to provide her the hope to move forward, to guide her in the right direction to follow. She felt that there was only one way to go - down - and that she was moving there fast.

When will things get easy? She looked to take a seat, and saw that it was graffitied with two words - 'I promise' - what do you promise? she wondered angrily. A promise to myself? A promise to God?

A small boy interrupted Chloe as she was contemplating her confusion. He looked no more than 10, and carried a soccer ball in his left arm.

"Hey!" he said, curiously looking at Chloe. His cap tipped lightly to the left, and he had a small scratch on his cheek.

"Hi," Chloe replied, raising her eyebrows as a form of recognition. She felt irritated of having been interrupted, but at the same time, she knew she had no right to let the boy be aware of the demons that were playing games in her mind. He was an innocent child, just seeking conversation.

"What have you got there?" he asked, pointing to the cylinder containing her drawings.

Just a pile of worthless paintings. she thought in her head as she held the container in her hands. They felt like they were burning in her fingers, aching to be let go of, but she couldn't let them go. Something told her to hold onto them.

"Some pictures I painted," she replied timidly.

"Can I see?" he asked, "I really like pictures."

Chloe looked to the young child. His innocent demeanor was so pure and enchanting that it spoke to her through his eyes, which twinkled with excitement. Light blue eyes with slivers of grey. He smiled a goofy grin, with teeth too big for his mouth. He was still growing into them. It was evident that all he cared about was sitting right there next to her, and being able to look at her pictures. It was what was going to make him happy, and who was she to stop this little child from being happy, just because she was unhappy?

"Of course, they aren't very good though…" Chloe replied as she opened the case and pulled out what she once considered her masterpieces.

"Don't say that." the boy shook his head as he replied. "My mama says that everything in this world is beautiful in its own way. Just because something isn't good, doesn't mean it's not beautiful."

Chloe smiled empathically. Why was it so hard to see things clearly sometimes, she wondered. Here, this small boy was able to summarize life in a matter of a sentence, and it was so simple, yet she seemed to forget it all the time, constantly tripping over herself when in fact she was strong enough to walk proudly, with her head held high.

"Oh wow! I like this one!" he said, as she revealed the first drawing. It was her favorite picture too. It was a sketch of a small lake that ran through the countryside, with horses and cows standing in a meadow. It was her grandmothers' farm that her family would go to on the holidays. She would spend hours lying by that lake, staring up at the sky and making animals from the clouds with her sister. Sometimes she would talk to the horses and cows and pick flowers. She liked the way she captured that moment, that feeling in the drawing - a vision of peace and serenity. But after her meeting with Mrs. Salters she wondered if she was the only one who felt that way from looking at it. Maybe she held an emotional attachment to the place as opposed to executing the idea from the colors.

"It looks like a place I'd like to go to." the young boy said smiling as he moved onto the next painting.

The next picture was intense. It was a painting of the first time a boy broke Chloe's heart. She had experimented with charcoal on paper. She had felt as though the charcoal represented the fire that had once burned inside her heart, a flame holding tight for the 15-year-old boy in her class. And the moment he told her he liked her friend, she extinguished it herself, pouring boiling water on the flames until they suffocated beneath, and all that was left was this burnt out charcoal, that she used to pull out whatever emotion she held left for this foolish lost love.

"I like the smokey layers up top over here." he said, as he pointed to the top right corner. "And here." he continued, enthusiastically. "I like the way this line moves as though it has a mind of its own."

Chloe giggled. "Thanks." she said. She had never thought of her lines as being individual and having a life of their own, but what the boy said made perfect sense.

"I could stare at this for hours." he replied. "There's so many stories in here."

"Do you like it?" she asked feeling the emotion of sadness override her mind as she looked at the picture. All the feelings of hurt that she felt from the rejection came flooding back, and piled on top of her recent experience of being rejected by the school.

"Very much. I kind of like dark pictures, is that weird?" he asked Chloe honestly.

"Not at all. I like dark pictures too." she replied with a wink and smile.

As he turned the paper to look at the third picture, a bus pulled up.

"That's my bus," he said, as he quickly stood up and handed the drawings back to Chloe.

"Thank you for showing me your pictures, I really liked them." He smiled.

"Thank you for asking." Chloe replied, taking the drawings from his hands as he ran to the door of the bus.

"Wait!" Chloe yelled, standing up and running to the young boy. "I want you to have this."

She handed him the charcoal drawing that he said he liked. The emotion she felt when holding the picture felt too strong, and she wanted to forget about that chapter in her life and move on. By releasing the picture from her hands it felt like a metaphor: that she was also releasing herself from the pain that she once held onto. It was the pain that she used as a point of reference to define herself. She didn't need it anymore. It was her way of cleansing herself from the past and making way for the future.

"Wow, thanks lady." he replied, a smitten smile on his face and a twinkle in his blue-grey eyes. "I guess it's my lucky day." He nodded as he walked into the bus.

"Mine too." Chloe replied, and watched as the bus drive away. The young boy sat to the front and hung out the window, waving her goodbye.

Chloe's bus arrived next, and she got on, feeling a tiny bit better than before. She got off at the hospital on her way home. Although she really just wanted to go home and feel sorry for herself, it had been two weeks since the accident, and Chloe knew that a small visit to let Ashley know how the interview went would mean a lot to her. And in an awful way, she knew that seeing her sister in the hospital bed unable to move would help put everything into perspective. She was healthy and her sister was lucky to be alive.

When she arrived to her sister's bed, Dr. Clive was visiting. Chloe tried to hold it together in front of him, but the moment she looked at her sister, tears quickly started to fall down her cheeks. She felt embarrassed, ashamed and stupid for trying to achieve something and then hopelessly failing. The doctor politely excused himself as Chloe stormed in, unable to hide the discouragement she felt.

"Chloe, Chloe calm down." her sisters soft voice purred as she reached out to touch Chloe's hand. But it was too late, the tears were already falling and it was impossible to stop them.

"It's just such a slap in the face!" Chloe said to her sister as her tears now changed to anger as she listened to herself retell the story of what had happened with Mrs. Salters. "Does the universe have a better plan? What else can I do but paint? I can't live another life. I love painting with my body and soul. I love it so much! I don't want to give it up when I am so passionate about it."

"Well, listen to what you are saying! Keep at it! Why stop?" Ashley asked. The bruises on her forehead had now begun to heal, and she scratched them often, saying the healing made them itchy.

"Because I need to make money from it and if no one thinks it is worth money, how do I keep going? How do I survive in a world that relies on money?" Chloe complained in response, and she thought about how she wished that money didn't exist, and she was free to explore her passion as she wished.

"Okay, so plan A didn't work, let's switch to plan B." Ashley sat up straight as she replied to her sister, delivering the advice in her usual authoritative manner. It was this kind of reaction that drove Chloe a little mad because of course it was easy for her sister to say this. She had a clear vision of her goals and the direction on how to reach them. Sometimes Chloe found it was easier to just complain and cry. Why did her sister always have to be right!

"I don't have a plan B!" Chloe snapped back, angry and irritated now, although she knew her sister was only trying to help. "I feel strange. Like I'm constantly floating in between two lives: one where I am, and the other where I want to be."

Chloe was pacing around the hospital bed and from side to side, as though the energy within her couldn't let her sit still. She felt hopelessly lost.

"Chloe, it's going to be okay. It's only one persons' opinion. It's only your ego that's been hurt, but you haven't been physically touched." she said as she looked to her sister. "Take some deep breaths, come on."

Ashley took long deep breaths, and Chloe reluctantly followed. By the end of the fifth breath, Chloe had calmed down. She realized that she had been overreacting and her tears began to stop. But the confusion and despair didn't leave her thoughts.

"I just don't know what I'm going to do now. I thought this was the right path, but I feel like I'm being pushed off track. Is it a sign?" Chloe asked as she looked out the window, wishing that she would see a real sign.

"Just because you are being redirected it doesn't mean you have to give up all hope of pursuing your dreams. You are always going to have things going against you. But are you really going to give up over this one small thing?"

Chloe nodded.

"Well, Chloe, I don't know if what I am going to say is going to calm you or make you feel worse, but yes, life does get harder. But you know what? You get stronger! Your mind gets stronger and things that you didn't think you could handle now, later become something so easy. And the challenges are new and fresh each time. Sometimes you wonder how it is even possible that it could be that way. But you need to stay positive. Look at me and all I've been through, but through it I've stayed positive!"

Her sister was right, always right. The wise older sibling had done it again, and Chloe envied her sister for the wisdom she possessed. She didn't know it was possible to be able to hold such higher knowledge. She sat eagerly, soaking up her sister's advice.

"If you believe life is going to be hard, it will be hard. If you seek beauty in everything, then beauty will be shown. But you need to pursue the quest for the right path. If you take no path, no path is going to be taken for you. Sometimes I used to let fate take too much control of my life, and yes, to an extent, it will override my plans. But at the same time, you need to start somewhere and you need to open a door, and then fate will either close it, or encourage you to open a different door. But if you don't open that door, no door will be opened and will you stand there in an empty room by yourself with no way in and no way out."

Chloe had the weirdest image inside her mind of what her sister was saying. She could see herself locked inside a tiny room with dark purple walls. It was windowless and had three doors. She had to chose a door, but as she tried to decide, her mind began to wander. She closed her eyes and chose the door on her right, opened it up, and braced herself for whatever lay on the other side. Everything she wanted was there! She stood looking at a seaside, along a small green grassy beach. On the side of the beach next to her stood an easel with a blank canvas and oil paints.

"I want to be a professional artist." Chloe said, as she opened her eyes and relayed what she had seen.

Her sister smiled with gratitude and relief that Chloe had finally chosen to listen to herself.

"Great, I'm very glad to hear that," Ashely said. "Now, do you know what you have to do?"

"No. But I'm going to find out." Chloe replied, as she kissed her sister goodbye.

But by the time Chloe arrived home, all the good advice from her sister had disappeared into the vortex of her consciousness. All her friends were all enjoying their university, and here she was, still at home, rejected from art school, and still doing nothing. She had tried to rationalize that she was still figuring things out, but it was six weeks since school had finished and she still had no direction. Well, she thought she did, but she was wrong. She wasn't good enough, she heard a voice inside say again.

It was too easy for her to fall down the hole of self-doubt - a lonely journey for an insecure soul, desperately trying to seek approval from others. But what was it that she wanted? A simple pat on the back to say "Yes, you did a good job". When it was completely impossible for everyone to like the same thing. "Everywhere you look," Chloe reasoned, "You see different tastes in everything- in music, clothes, food, cities and countries, the list continues for an eternity, and never does anyone agree on the same thing." So she asked herself, "Why stop at one bad comment? At one woman at one art school telling her, "No this isn't the right fit for our university." She began to analyze her options. 1) she wasn't meant to pursue her dream of being an artist 2) seek alternative ways to be successful as a painter. 3) play the role of a victim and feel sorry for herself.

She laughed at how miserable she had managed to make herself. It was either laugh or cry and she had cried enough for today, she thought.

But as the days passed the urge to escape from her life seemed to overtake her thoughts. The alluring idea of leaving everything she had ever known and starting all over again, by herself without any attachments, no memories, no emotions. She wondered if it would be easier. Not loving or caring for anyone. Then she realized that by going it alone and not loving or caring for anyone, she would also be not herself, for the people around her completed her life. Why was she so very angry at that woman at the university, someone she had never met before, someone who would probably never come into her life again after those unbearably awkward 15 minutes? She still had to see the positive, that this women awoke something inside of her. She exposed a side of truth to herself that she didn't know existed. She realized that the truth was Mrs. Sanders comments had revealed to Chloe a previously hidden sense of insecurity, and a bruised ego. It was a moment in time when she saw her life in a different light. Even so, Chloe didn't want to see it. She preferred to hold on to her bruised ego a little bit longer. So, instead, she applied for a job at the local cafe, deciding that her new mission would be to save up some money, and then go traveling to escape her haunting reality.

Six

A Difference Of Opinion

Chloe didn't mind her new job at the local cafe. She had been working there for over month now, and it was easy for her. Her life had become a simple routine: wake up, work, sleep, repeat. Her parents were happy that she was doing something with her life, although she felt like she was pitied by her friends. And she was jealous of the fraternity and sorority parties and the overall social life that all her friends who were at university seemed to enjoy. Even though she was invited to the social events and occasionally went, she always felt out of place. It was like she was visiting a foreign country and no one there spoke English. Everyone else had their own lingo of university talk, and she just wasn't a part of it, no matter how much she tried to be.

And her self-confidence was starting to decline. She could see that when she told people her new plan of saving and traveling, there was a look of judgement on their faces, and she felt it herself. It was as if she was wasting her life away with no purpose or direction. "No," she thought, "I'm not wasting my life! I have a plan, and I know that my life will be enriched from my travels."

But she forgot about her dreams for awhile as her work at the cafe grew in days and hours. The paintbox that used to sit proudly in the corner of her room was now hidden in the closet. Although Chloe still felt as though she could hear it calling out to her sometimes, she was too scared to get it out, scared that if she opened it an emotion greater than she could handle would take over her. And now she had learned how to fill the gap she had within herself from not painting, she was filling it up with her new love for Ricardo.

From the moment she met Ricardo, a young Italian chef at the cafe where she worked at, she was distracted from the worries of her old life. Ricardo was very interesting. He was different from anyone she had ever met. He spoke with a thick Italian accent, and wore a denim biker jacket with a red flannelette collar. Even though that fashion had expired many years before, he somehow pulled it off. And his body was covered in tattoos - too many to count. She loved how they expressed his own individualism.

Over the last five weeks, they had made eye contact 20 times, and they had had a total of eight conversations (although, two of the conversations were related to work, so Chloe wasn't really sure if they counted). But it didn't matter, because she could feel the chemistry blaze between them like electric lightning in the sky.

On Tuesdays, Thursdays and Saturdays their shifts coincided, and Chloe couldn't wait until those days came around. She always spent the day before trying on her outfit and playing with beauty masks as though 'ready' for the moment that he was to ask her out. And finally, that day came, on a Saturday afternoon at 4pm when she arrived for her evening shift.

"What time do you finish today?" Ricardo asked, as he wiped his strong hands with a wash cloth in the back room next to her.

His hands were always covered in something. Chloe always noticed, and she adored it. To her it meant that he was passionate about his cooking and it showed a side of determination in him. She often secretly watched him from the backroom as he was working in the kitchen. Even the way he chopped and prepared the cuisine was interesting to her; he certainly had an international flare to his cooking and it fascinated Chloe.

"Nine o'clock." Chloe replied, smiling sweetly as her heart began to beat fast while she looked into his eyes.

He easily returned her gaze, then looked to the ceiling as though thinking about his words carefully. It was just long enough to tantalize Chloe and confuse her about what to do next. She sometimes caught herself waiting for his next words, and had to tell herself to go back to work, or something along the same lines.

"Let's have a drink after?" he asked as he raised his thick eyebrows, and stroked his beard on the side of his jawline.

Chloe nodded in response and quickly looked away. It wasn't that she was trying to play it cool, it was simply that he made her lose all control. Her thoughts became muddled, and she felt as though her breathing made a loud hissing noise. This was the moment she had finally waited for. A date with the man she had been lusting over for weeks. And as she jumped up and down inside her mind, her first thought was - I can't wait to tell Ashley!

But as nine o'clock came around, he had not followed through with a place to meet. Chloe stood in the back of the cafe, tormented as to whether to wait, or turn around and go home. She hurriedly called Ashley from the bathroom, hoping that her crush couldn't hear her.

"What do I do?" Chloe asked, looking at herself in the mirror. She had already applied fresh make-up, under the assumption that the date was happening. But as soon the opportunity presented itself for Chloe to feel insecure, there she was again, her confidence diminishing as quickly as she could blink.

"Be confident Chloe!" her sister argued back in the phone. "Just go and find out what's happening, that's better than waiting around, right?" Chloe nodded on the other end of the phone. "And you're a busy girl, you have things to do. If he has other plans, you do too. It's easy. Don't complicate it."

"But what if my meddling changes our arrangements? Shouldn't I just act cool and let him come to me?"

"To an extent yes, but this isn't really chasing when he initiated it. If it does amount to something, your meddling or not meddling isn't going to change the outcome."

Chloe could imagine Ashley's face as she provided her sisterly advice over the phone. And she could almost see the way she would stare at Chloe, it was her way of pushing the truth into her sister. And of course she was right, she was always right. Chloe giggled in response, agreeing that she was being over-analytical. Then she hopped off the phone and walked right up to the kitchen.

"Hey! I was just about to find you." Ricardo said smoothly as he took his chef's hat off. "Are you ready to go?" He raised his eyebrows in a mischievous manner, and the scent of his cologne breezed over toward her.

Chloe nodded in reply, she couldn't speak. She wanted to, but the words felt like they were stuck in her throat and she felt as though her entire face was burning red as it lit up with excitement. And then her heart began to beat so loudly, she wondered if he could hear it.

"Let's go to a bar nearby. There's some live music playing tonight." Ricardo suggested as he picked up his trademark denim jacket and opened up the door for Chloe to walk through.

Chloe tried hard not to imagine wearing the jacket, but she couldn't help doing so. The thought overrode her swirling emotions and she smiled as she walked with him down the street. The moon in the sky hung low, and as she looked up she made a small wish on the first star she saw. Let everything happen for my greater good. She whispered. As they walked in silence along the dark street, she played with questions in her mind as to what to say next. She never usually got nervous when it came to boys, but for some reason, Ricardo shook her up completely.

"What kind of music do you like?" she finally asked in an attempt to start a conversation, since not much was said since they left the cafe, and the silence had begun to make Chloe feel uncomfortable.

"I'm showing you tonight, this is my favorite kind of music." He smiled with charismatic charm. Chloe felt as though he was inviting her into a part of his life, and she felt happy, knowing that she was learning something special about him.

"What time do they start?" she asked, although she didn't really care. She just wanted to keep the conversation going, that, and to hear the Italian accent glide over his words. It didn't matter what he said, she was mesmerized with his presence. And the sound of his voice created a soft humming sound in her ear.

"They should've started by the time we arrive." Ricardo replied, as he wrapped his jacket around his shoulders, styling his clothes confidently.

As they walked together, Chloe would casually look in his direction and although she didn't say anything to him, she would often find him watching her. To Chloe, it was reassurance that the attraction between them was mutual.

They arrived at the bar with a two-member band already on the stage, and a small crowd of twenty-something-year-old people sitting on various tables.

"What do you want to drink?" he asked, ordering himself a beer from the waiter. But he didn't wait for her answer, and instead, he paid for his own drink, and started to walk toward the closest table.

"I'll just have a glass of orange juice." Chloe said to the waiter. She didn't really enjoy drinking, rather felt as though it blocked her thoughts and that she acted foolishly when she drank alcohol. Plus, she hadn't felt like it since Ashley's accident due to a drunk driver.

Chloe joined Ricardo at the table while they listened to the music. It was two young men playing drums and a guitar. They played an acoustic song with softly spoken words over the top. She felt as though the cords of music they played moved through her body like poetry and it lingered in the air above her, waiting to be absorbed. She liked it, and it made her like Ricardo even more, because if he too liked this intense music, he might, like her, be a deep thinker.

"Do you miss Italy?" she asked, brushing her hair behind her shoulders as she moved closer to be able to hear him over the music.

"Yeah, but I chose this life. All I care about is traveling." he replied as he took a sip of his beer.

"And cooking? Is it your passion?" Chloe asked, resting her elbows on the table as she listened to him.

"Not really, I just work enough to survive and move on to the next place." He shrugged his shoulders as though that was what life was all about.

Even though a part of Chloe wished he cared more about his cooking, so that her assumption about his passion would have been correct, she was more intrigued with his carefree attitude and his worldly experience. The thought of the unknown excited her, and she hoped that perhaps traveling might serve the purpose that she was looking for - that maybe, she would find her true calling in foreign lands.

"That's what I want to do too." Chloe gushed, already thinking that perhaps they could travel together.

But to her dismay, he didn't comment. Instead, he responded with "cool" as he raised his bushy eyebrows and turned his face back to the music.

She looked around the room. Couples were kissing and friends were hanging out and laughing, engaged in conversation. And here she was, sitting next to her ultimate crush, but she felt as though the space between her and Ricardo was lacking any interaction. So she casually tried to start conversation again.

"Where are you heading to next?" she asked, tucking her hair behind her ears and showing off the new earrings she had bought, especially for this occasion.

"I'm going to Bali after here," he replied, taking another swig of his beer and continuing to look at the guitarist.

"Me too!" Chloe said excitedly. "Well it's either Bali or Thailand, I'm not sure where yet. I just know that I want to take off soon."

And it was true. Asia was the closest to Australia, and definitely the cheapest for her to travel to. She was almost three weeks away from having enough money to buy her plane ticket. Although she knew she wouldn't leave until Ashely was out of the hospital, it felt nice to plan ahead for once.

But as Chloe told him her travel ideas, Ricardo just nodded and smiled in reply and turned back to the music as his form of entertainment. When the song had finished, he casually grazed his hand over hers, looked deeply into her eyes and asked her, "Do you want to come back to my place and hang out?"

Even though the thought of kissing Ricardo was exactly what Chloe had dreamed about for the last 5 weeks of work, she didn't want to do it like this. Not from a boring night in a dingy bar with a guy who showed barely any interest in her as a person. And as Chloe later recalled the evening that they had, she realized that he didn't once ask her a question about herself. Not once. Even when she shared something about herself, without being asked, he didn't share the same enthusiasm as she did with his own inner thoughts. It was obvious from his playful charm that Ricardo knew he was good looking, and perhaps his aloofness was appealing to other girls . . . But not to her. In that moment of her telling him that she was planning to go traveling as well, right after he had said that his next stop was Asia, there was no talk about her coming with him, not even for a visit. She realized the truth of his intentions toward her, which were nothing more than a casual fling. She couldn't help but be disappointed by his lack of interest. Not that she had a right to be upset, but still, disappointment felt appropriate. What was the point of their night out? What was he doing with her? Was he dangling the idea of a fling while he continued to pursue his own dreams and fulfill his own goals?

Chloe realized that even though she felt hurt by his not wanting to include her in his travel plans, perhaps he was showing her something in herself that was being neglected. Perhaps he was showing her how he was determined to follow his dreams of traveling despite money being an issue, despite his need to constantly move around without any true ties anywhere.

And even though she felt rejected yet again, perhaps it was the push that she needed. She finished her orange juice and said she needed to go home. She told him a fake family emergency had occurred, and that she would see him at work tomorrow. He didn't seem too phased by her abrupt departure and ordered another beer. She smiled and waved goodbye, but she secretly wished she didn't have to face him at work ever again.

Seven

Garden Of Life

When Chloe got home she took a long hot bath and changed into warm clothes. She tried to make sense of the overload of emotions that had quickly come crashing down onto her. She couldn't help but feel upset. It was as though nothing was going right in her life. She constantly felt like everything and everyone was against her, that everything was just one great big disappointment after the other.

She sat upright on the head of her bed and set her meditation timer, ready for her meditation. She knew it was the answer to her uncontrollable emotions getting the better of her mind, and meditation helped her see the situation from a different perspective, reminding her to be patient with the journey of life. As she closed her eyes to delve deep inside herself, she wondered, why she had waited so long to do this when it had always created such a beautiful, profound experience afterwards. She felt more in tune with herself, more accepting of herself after she meditated. She had discovered a new way to come home to herself, but it had been weeks since she had meditated, and even longer since she had called upon her Spirit Guides.

She began with deep breathing as instructed by her sister. And in those few moments that she spent peacefully breathing she felt inspired. Her overload of thoughts slowly diminished and she felt herself swirling in a circle. A compass of black surrounded her, and slowly, as the spinning began to stop, colors overtook her senses, flashing in spots and squares and shapes of every kind. The colors then turned into shapes, and the shapes into people, animals and places. She finally rested in the same place she had been in before. 'The meeting place'. She stood on top of the hill with the long road, the giant tree on the left, the soft pebbles on the ground and the tall grass. The sun had not risen, it was dawn and the atmosphere was misty. It wasn't difficult to see right in front of her, but it was hard to see far away.

After a short time time, Sam appeared once again. this time he wore a blue silk kimono, and traditional Japanese wooden sandals on his feet. He nodded to her and the same feeling of comfort they had shared on her previous visit overtook them both. In this moment that they shared, Chloe forgot everything of her life back home. The sadness she felt for her ill sister and the fear of her own limiting beliefs all vanished when she was with him. It was strange. The energy between them just blossomed like a flower, constantly opening, the petals forever changing their shapes and colors. So beautiful! It felt so calming, yet at the same time exciting - a non-stop process of transformation.

"I don't remember why I came here." Chloe finally said as they stood together.

"Come." he said, directing her to walk with him up the hill. "At the top of this hill is your Garden of Life at this present moment."

Chloe walked side by side with Sam up the hill. It stretched out longer than she expected and the pebbles on the ground began to get thicker as she reached the top. She held no fear inside herself, rather, eagerness to see what awaited them at the top.

"This is your Garden of Life." Sam announced as he gestured to the empty garden in front of them. It was a big, wooden-fenced rectangular garden, full of dried hay and a little compost. There are too many empty holes in the ground and too much empty space, Chloe thought, and she felt empty staring at it. There were no flowers, no grass, no plants or trees. It wasn't an inviting environment to walk through, and Chloe felt deeply saddened that she had created this world for herself.

She stood next to the closest hole and touched the edge.

"This hole represents your self-love and self-confidence." Sam said as he watched Chloe mourn in silence.

"And the this one?" she asked, walking to the second hole, looking inside the vast empty space.

"This is your life's purpose. You are not listening to yourself."

"I cannot hear myself!" Chloe replied angrily, but the notion of anger did not exist in this world and it disappeared before it even tried to come out. Her words were spoken softly and neutralized, and the self-pity she once felt had disappeared too. She only wanted to better herself and create a harmonious environment that would enable her to blossom within.

"I want to plant seeds and water this garden." Chloe said as she stared at the mess in front of her, and as she spoke of her desires, they manifested in front of her being.

In her left hand she now held a seed, and in her right hand, a bucket of water. She leapt to the first empty space, and placed the seed deeply into it, and while doing so she wished love and light to grow within it. She pushed a pile of dirt that had now appeared next to the hole and filled it up. Then, she poured the water from the bucket slowly into the hole, and watched as the dirt rose with the water, seeping quickly into the ground, wanting to refresh itself with a vibration of new energy.

Once satisfied with her planting, she moved onto the next one. And then the next one, and the next one after that, and she didn't stop. She moved so quickly she felt as though she had multiple versions of herself working at the same time and continued until she couldn't move any further.

After she had caressed each empty vessel with love and a seed of new birth, she rested and stood back with Sam to look at what she had created.

Sam waved to the sky, and the sun rose high above them, and as it did, the plants began to blossom, and beautiful grass grew. Chloe could hear birds chirping, and butterflies began flying around them. She lifted her hand and fluttered her fingers, as though mimicking a waterfall of rain. And together with the help of Sam, she created a rain to fall and water the garden once more. In the strong bright sunlight the flowers grew tall and beautiful and colorful, and the animals and birds quickly followed their lead. She smiled to Sam.

"You have the power to change your garden for better or worse anytime you wish." he said.

"I want to shower it with love and positivity always. Look how beautiful this feels." Chloe closed her eyes, feeling the warmth of the sun on her face and the cleansing energy from the rain that now surrounded them.

She opened her eyes and was drawn to a flower. It was full of pink tulip petals, soft and delicate to touch.

"This flower represents happiness." Chloe heard a voice speak inside.

"How do I get it?" she asked.

Sam came and stood next to her. "Continue on your path, keep doing what you are doing and never give up. Creating magic is what makes you truly happy."

"But I don't know my direction." Chloe replied sadly.

"Yes you do." Sam said, but his mouth didn't open as he responded. Instead, Chloe felt as though the voice was coming from her heart.

"You mean my painting?"

Sam nodded.

"Never stop creating your beauty. Keep your magic alive and it will continue to feed your soul."

The words Sam spoke resonated strongly with Chloe, and as she agreed with this simple truth, she realized she was crazy to have ever thought otherwise.

"Can we explore this garden?" Chloe asked, as the grass around them had now grown higher, and the flowers kept blossoming, and the animals kept reproducing. What would have taken years to evolve on Earth, took mere seconds in this magical place. Sam nodded, and together they wandered through the tall grass leaves and endless flowering plants that now marked the edge of the roads like a fence. And as she graced through the tall grass, the whiskers of their tips tickled her skin. The grass looked as though it extended for miles, she looked around, trying to find an end goal to be reached, but there was none. And so she stopped in her tracks and looked to Sam, who looked back at her, his big eyes revealing his loving heart. The outer edge of his body somehow disappeared into the surroundings around him, and all Chloe could see was the auric field energy of his heart, a bouncing light of white and gold in front of her.

"Shall we sit?" she asked, ignoring the fact that she couldn't see his body, it didn't matter - she still felt his presence.

They sat down on the ground, right where they were, with the tall grass hovering over their heads. To the right of where she sat between two long stalks of green grass, there was a beautiful spider web. So intricately woven, so delicately created that she was utterly mesmerized. Small droplets of morning dew hung to the edges of the silk web, like jewels, glistening in the sun. The edges of the web stretched out with unbalanced harmony. Yet, the rawness and unevenness was perfectly synchronized to catch the spider's prey. The pattern appeared like a maze and every piece held great importance. One thread was produced to come after and to connect back to the piece that was spun before. Neither could stand without each other, and with this web the spider, a master engineer, had manifested its own glory. Slowly, and carefully, with great patience, an idea came into fruition, from inside the spiders' mind.

As Chloe looked to Sam, she could feel his intention through his energy, and as prompted, she looked back to the spiders' web, with great determination to understand its message.

"Look at the time it took for the spider took to create its art." Sam said as he pointed to the spider.

"Everything takes time, but time is obsolete. Eventually you will get there. Sometimes it will speed up and at other times feel as if it was moving at a turtles' pace, but you mustn't give up on understanding and appreciating the simple pleasures of life. If you find what it is that makes you happy and you do this every day, then you will have created a beautiful life for yourself."

Chloe nodded with admiration for the spider and relief for having met Sam. She could feel the burning desire inside of her to do as he suggested and take the time to build her life as she desired. To create the life she had always wanted.

Then the sound of the chimes from her alarm clock drifted through the space where she sat, and slowly, Sam and the world she imagined drifted away too.

"I will come visit soon." she promised, smiling at Sam and thanking him for his gift.

When Chloe woke up she felt as though she had literally come back into her body. It was a strange feeling, as though she had opened her eyes for the very first time. She felt empowered, motivated and ready as she reflected upon the vision she'd had of how beautifully the spider had created its web. It made her think of her desire to be an artist.

She wondered what strong, stable steps she could take to make her dream into a reality. She knew she could make it real but that it would take time, but time she had. Everyone has time, she thought. And through her dream of being a self-employed artist she could see the steps in place that she needed to take. How she would need to be aware of her surroundings, learn the art world and understand the mindset of the customers who would buy it. It wouldn't just be a matter of luck - she needed to build networks and attract the clients. As much as she desired to retreat inside her creative hub, she knew she needed to expand and push herself out of her comfort zone to learn from those who had successfully walked the artists' way before her. She knew she had what it took to succeed. Strength and determination like that of the spider, to never give up. No matter what obstacle stood in her way she would succeed. Even if she was the last one standing, she would succeed.

She picked up her notebook laying next to the bed and started to write a plan. It started with a one week plan, then a one month plan, then a one year plan and ended with a five year plan. She just kept writing and writing, and planning how to manifest and create her most desirable future of an ideal world that would make her the happiest to live in. She wrote down the little steps which lead to the big steps and understood that although it would take time she would be happy every step of the way because it would lead her that much closer to her dream.

"I'm not going to spend my money on traveling as I originally thought." Chloe said to her parents the next morning over breakfast. Her mother and father looked at each other, confused, and wondering what she was going to say next. "I want to buy some new art supplies, and start painting again." Chloe told them as she sat them down to explain her plan. "I'm thinking of trying to get a job at an art gallery. Even if it's just an internship to start with, I'll be happy."

Her parents paused before replying, and Chloe wondered if in fact she had their support. But she finally felt the confidence within that even if she didn't, it wasn't going to stop her, for she felt the strength she needed within her own self.

"Chloe it's so beautiful to see you have direction and goals once again. We support you 100%!" her father said as he and her mother both nodded. "You are very talented and we believe in you."

And from just this simple support from her family, Chloe felt strength in her essence, and a little bit more confidence in her brush strokes.

"I'm going to research every art gallery in town and submit my resume." she continued, showing her resume to her parents. "Can you please look it over and let me know if it's okay? I stayed up all night doing it."

Her parents looked it over, and then looked to one another and smiled, nodding their heads together in agreement. "It looks great Chloe. Make sure you go in person to these art galleries, ask to see the owner or at least the manager and hand it to whoever that is, okay?" her father said in an authoritative tone.

"Yes, yes! First impressions are the most important." her mother added. "And add a cover letter about why you want to work for them. Tell them how it's inline with your aspirations. This is always a great help."

Chloe smiled with enthusiasm and she jumped up and down like an excited child, ready to take the next step. She felt more determined than ever and ready to research the list of art galleries she would apply to.

"I'm going to go to the hospital and tell Ashley about it. I've been meaning to give her that painting I made her as well." Chloe said, as she remembered the turtle painting she made when Ashley first went into the hospital. She had packed it away along with her dreams, but now it was time to bring it back out into the light.

"Sure, I'll give you a lift. I need to go to the supermarket anyway." her mother said, standing and patting Chloe on the back, giving her a little nudge of support.

The hospital felt different each time Chloe went. Every time a little bit brighter, every time a little bit happier. Dr. Clive was sitting next to Ashley when she arrived. She stood in the doorway silently watching them converse. Ashley was staring intently at the doctor, listening, talking, and giggling. Chloe loved to see her that way. She hadn't seen such a beautiful smile on her sister's face in years. Was it due to her recovery, or was it something more? She wondered.

"Chloe!" Ashley shrieked with excitement. She was almost back to her regular self. The scars on her face had completely healed, and the color had seeped back into her cheeks.

"I'm not interrupting, am I?" Chloe smiled mischievously, she still loved to tease her sister after all.

"Not at all." the doctor replied as he moved back towards the door. "I'll let your sister tell you the good news." he continued as he smiled wholeheartedly.

He turned to leave, but not before looking at Ashley one last time before walking through the door.

"Chloe you brought me the painting!" Ashley said excitedly in a giddy school girl kind of voice as she pointed to the painting Chloe held in her hands.

"Whoa, hold on a minute. First of all, tell me: what was that was all about?" she demanded, pointing to the doctor. "Are you and…?"

"Well, kind of, yeah." Ashley smiled, looking away nervously. "We've been speaking every day, and he's so sweet and smart."

"And, do you like him?" Chloe put her hands on her hips as she asked, slightly demanding to know the answer. She was a little bit confused, but not surprised, because of course her sister would be able to turn any situation around from the negative to the positive.

"I just connect so well with his Eastern philosophy of life and his Indian upbringing." Ashley gushed as her eyes opened wide, and her smile mirrored the same openness. "And he just asked me out for a proper date." Chloe could tell she was very happy and excited.

"Oh, I'm so happy for you!"

"Thanks! But that wasn't the good news!" Ashley smiled again, laughing quietly to herself for holding it in.

"It wasn't?" Chloe asked as she placed the painting on the corner of the table.

"He also said that I can finally go home!"

"Ashley that's amazing!" Chloe squealed as she leapt into her sisters arms and cuddled her tightly. She could feel the bones still strong in her body, and uttered a big sigh of relief for how much everything could change in just a few weeks.

"When?"

"He said maybe by the weekend."

"What a wonderful turn of events this has been!" Chloe said as they laughed at the irony of the situation.

"I know!" she agreed. "Now, show me your painting!"

"I don't remember painting it of course." Chloe said as she lifted the painting to the base of the bed.

"Oh Chloe, it's incredible! I have shivers! It's exactly what I saw when I had my out of body experience." Ashley spoke with tears in her eyes as she reflected on her experience that felt so real, yet unable to be explained in words.

"What else happened when you were unconscious? Do you remember?" Chloe asked awkwardly. It's not that they hadn't talked about the accident, but the focus was always on how to get better, and future plans to move it along. But now that things were changing, it finally felt like the appropriate time to ask.

"I just remember the feeling of knowing. I can't remember too many visions, just visiting you, and I saw lots of different colors. I remember the feeling I had when you, mom and dad would visit. I could feel you here, did you know that?"

"How did you know?"

"I could just feel it. The energy felt different, like I was submerged in a warm pool of water. I felt nurtured and safe, supported and surrounded by all of your love. It was beautiful."

Ashley closed her eyes as she relived the moment and shared her thoughts. The words flowed through her effortlessly, and she painted a picture of how divinely connected they all were - how for a brief moment in time she was able to experience something so profound, so real and truthful that it put everything in her life into perspective. She now had a great appreciation for her life, with no fear of the future, no worries from the past, and she was able to focus her attention on just the present moment despite any apparent obstacles. And that present moment was sitting in her hospital room with her sister, sharing their time together by simply listening and sharing stories.

Eight

The Spider's Web

On Friday morning, Chloe set off bright and early to visit the list of art galleries she had prepared. With her printed resumes in one hand, and a warm smile written on her face, she began her quest.

The first location didn't feel right. The physical setup of the gallery itself mismatched her style. It resembled an antique house as opposed to a more modern, minimalist style apartment. And the second location showcased sculptures, not particularly Chloe's favorite form of art. Still, she appreciated everything and with determination asked for a job, but neither galleries were hiring.

"You seem very sweet, child, but I am sorry, we have no vacancy at the moment." the older man who owned the next gallery replied, as he smiled with care in his cheeks. Chloe only had a few more left on her list, and she stared back at the man with tears in her eyes, uttering a big sigh and turning to walk out the door, having been rejected once more. "Why don't you try Mrs. Brasley's gallery across the road there?" he suggested, as though reading Chloe's dejection.

Chloe looked at her list, and saw that she didn't have a Mrs. Brasley's Gallery written down on it.

"Is it new? I don't have it on my list." Chloe replied as she peeked across the road.

"Yes, she only opened it a few weeks ago, and she might need some help. She's an artist herself."

Chloe thanked the old man, then crossed the street to Mrs. Brasley's gallery. She felt strange as she looked at the shopfront. It felt familiar somehow. Have I been there before? she wondered. The glass windows were wide and open, revealing a vast empty space with modern drawings on the walls, and small lights hovering above each frame to bring them to life. The style was very modern and Chloe was immediately intrigued.

The door was closed, but there was a small bell in front of it, to which Chloe rang.

"Hello." A friendly voice came to her through door. It belonged to a woman in her early 40's with dark red hair and small green glasses. "I don't open until midday, I'm sorry." she said, checking the time on her watch. "Oh it's only in fifteen minutes, do you want to come in and wait?"

"Yes please." Chloe nodded.

The interior walls were a stony grey, the concrete on the floor extended up high into the ceiling and at the very back of the gallery she saw an open window of pure glass, overlooking a beautiful garden full of lush trees and large plants. Chloe thought the garden was a wonderful contrast to the inside of the gallery, and she eagerly wanted to explore more.

"My name is Chloe, Mrs. Brasley, and I was actually wondering if you needed any help here, I heard you have just opened."

"Call me Veronica," the lady said as she smiled and looked at Chloe. "What do you want to do here?"

Chloe smiled back eagerly, showcasing her white teeth, "Anything you need. My passion is drawing and painting, and I'd like to get an understanding of what's involved on the selling side."

Veronica smiled, and pushed up her green glasses as she looked Chloe up and down.

"You remind me of myself when I was younger." she said, smiling warmly. "Tell me about the artwork that you create."

Chloe looked to the floor as she blushed.

"It's difficult to explain . . . Umm." She paused, as she relived the emotion of what she felt as she painted. "It's like an overload of information wanting to move through my body and stain the canvas in front of me, and I just can't control the urge, I need to release the energy. And then when I look, there it is, a piece of artwork in front of me. It has the power to take control of me. Does that make sense?"

Veronica laughed, as her eyes squinted behind her glasses. "It does, yes. Okay, well, how do you feel about an internship? You could work with me a couple of hours a day, unpaid, and as time goes on, if you prove your value, I will pay you."

Chloe wanted to jump up and down she was so excited. This was exactly what she wanted! And the art gallery was by far the most interesting of them all the ones she had visited.

"That would be amazing! I just want to learn as much as possible!" Chloe replied enthusiastically.

"You can start right now if you would like." Mrs. Brasley replied, opening her palms up and smiling in reply. Her lips smothered across her teeth and they rose up high, almost touching her nose.

"Do . . you want to read my resume?" Chloe asked, pulling out the piece of paper that she had used to define her achievements.

"No it's okay. I can read the kind of person you are, and I'm willing to take the chance."

Chloe smiled a heartfelt smile that she had never felt for a complete stranger before. And even though she wasn't getting paid, the experience was more valuable. It wasn't just a job in which she would answer calls and wipe down walls, she actually had an artist and an art gallery owner to look up to and learn from. She couldn't have asked for a better situation to have happened to her.

"Are any of these artworks yours?" Chloe asked, as she looked at the beautiful pictures around her.

"Yes, this is my latest work." Veronica said as she pointed to a charcoal picture that hung just above the office desk and to the left of where they were standing.

The charcoal imagery moved in lines and strong patterns. On one side the weight felt low to the ground, and to the right it lifted up high, as though something had magnetically pulled it to the top.

Chloe felt connected to the image, like it resembled that of her life, the constant waves of emotions that she seemed to ride upon. Sometimes she cruised with the water, skidding along gleefully with an open heart, excited to take on the next adventure. And other times, she felt suffocated beneath the weight of the water, drowning and wondering if she would ever resurface. Today, she realized that she had taught herself how to swim, and to control whatever waters life dealt her.

"It's really wonderful," Chloe replied happily, she loved to finally be around the things that inspired her.

"Thanks! Okay, it's time to change over the front window, I have something peculiar to put on one side. Will you help me please?"

Veronica brought out a newspaper-covered frame from the back room, and handed it to Chloe.

"Of course! Why is it so strange?" Chloe asked as she laid the wrapped picture on the table.

"Well, you see, I don't know who the artist is! So I want to put a little note beneath it - asking the artist to come forward. Our town's not that big you know."

The lady handed Chloe a small printed card that asked the artist to come forward. Chloe placed it on the table and helped Veronica take down the picture in the front window.

"Do you mind hanging it for me?"

"Not at all," Chloe replied as she carefully unwrapped the picture frame. "Where did you find it?"

"My son found it for me."

Chloe's whole body started to shiver as an eruption of heat exploded through her body, and as the last layer of paper was removed, her artwork was revealed. Tears welled deep within her eyes, but didn't release. They were forming from happiness.

"Um . . this is a weird coincidence." Chloe began as she blushed feverishly. "It was me who gave this to your son, this is my drawing."

Veronica's eyes popped out through her long eyelashes and she opened her mouth in shock. "It's . . . it's yours? And here you are. I can't believe it!"

"Yep, here I am." Chloe smiled awkwardly, excited but confused as to where the conversation would lead.

"You know, meetings like this don't just happen." Veronica said as she shook her head lightly. "I think you were meant to come here. This is too perfectly aligned."

Veronica moved closer to the image and smiled as she touched the edges of the picture frame lightly. The frame was a thin, gold wooden carving and it suited the image so well and Chloe couldn't believe how professional it looked.

She looked at Veronica as she stared at her picture. Chloe felt as though Veronica could feel the emotion of brokenness that the painting entailed for Chloe and that maybe Veronica could identify the same brokenness inside of herself.

"This painting sings so loudly in my heart." Veronica said as she attempted to grasp the right words to express the strong emotions moving through her. "It reminds me of different paths and moments passed by, of missed connections." She stared intently at the painting as she recalled a small piece inside of her heart that had never healed. It was an empty space of "What if?" What if she went down this path instead of that. What if she said yes. What if she tried again.

"Do you have anymore paintings?" she asked Chloe, smiling at the irony of the situation.

"Some, but, I don't think they are very good. I would love some help." Chloe replied nervously as she looked down to play with the rings on her fingers.

"Well, I'm sure they are better than you think. I would love to mentor you if you'd like?"

Chloe's heart began to beat fast with excitement, not nerves, just excitement. She finally felt like she had found a place where she could belong. A place that would help her be true to herself, and reveal the hidden creativities that lay dormant within her.

"Yes please." Chloe replied and nodded excitedly. She didn't feel like she had to hide her emotion with Veronica, nor in the art world. She could be free to be herself and be proud of it.

"Okay, this is the new plan. You can work in the shop for half a day, and the rest you will spend working on your artwork. And I want more, I need to see it now! I see great potential in you." Veronica replied with equal enthusiasm as her glasses began to slip off her nose.

Chloe felt an eruption of fireworks within her body. She was overloaded with joy and excitement. It was the sign she had been waiting for - something to help encourage her on her journey and push her onto the right path. She couldn't believe her luck. She couldn't understand how something so wonderful could happen to her.

"Can you bring them now? How far are you from your house?" Veronica smiled as she admired Chloe's work once more.

"About twenty minutes by bus."

"That's okay, why don't you catch a taxi, my treat. Go home, tell your parents you found a job and a mentor!" Veronica said as she opened the door for Chloe and handed her some cash.

And as Chloe walked through the door she felt different somehow. It was a distinct feeling of being guided and cared for that came from the universe that her sister used to describe, but that Chloe had never known before. She looked back to the art gallery before getting in the taxi and smiled with admiration for such a blessing to have come her way. As the taxi drove off she noticed a tiny black spider in the top right of the glass window. It was so high up it would normally have been difficult to see. But she saw it there silently spinning its web, carefully, patiently and meticulously creating something incredible. And even though the spider knew the web would take time to complete, it was unaware that its every action was weaving a path to its final destiny.

Instructions

How To Connect With Your Spirit Guides

PREPARATION:

It is important to have a regular meditation practice in place before meeting your Spirit Guides. You should already be comfortable mediating for a minimum of 15 minutes each day.

Once you have meditated regularly at the same time each day, and for a series of days in a row, it is time for you to meet your Spirit Guides!

Prepare your 'Meeting Place' by picturing a space in your mind that provides a feeling of safety and happiness. This place can be fictional or truly exist.

Before commencing your meditation, create a harmonizing environment around you (with the use of crystals, candles and/or meditation music). Next, protect your energy by envisioning a field of light energy around you, or with a prayer of protection. Clearly speak your intentions for the your meditation, with a request to meet your Spirit Guides.

MEETING YOUR SPIRIT GUIDES:

As you begin your meditation, allow at least 5 minutes of long drawn out breaths to relax into a deep state of consciousness, and after this time, imagine 'The Meeting Place' in your mind.

As you envision 'The Meeting Place' get comfortable in its surroundings.

Imagine the finer details of your surroundings, such as the colors and textures.

Make this 'Meeting Place' your own special place by exploring as much as possible. Continue to do this until your Spirit Guides arrive.

On the first encounter you may just see a flash of them; the second time you meditate you might sit together longer. And it might not be until the 7th or 20th time that you actually communicate with them.

Your Spirit Guides can appear in all kinds of shapes and sizes. They can be people or animals, or any type of object or visualization. You could have one, or two, or even thirty. They can communicate with you in many ways, such as through words, symbols, feelings, vibrations and sounds.

They are always with you, guiding you, protecting you and looking after you.

Be patient, grateful and always have an open heart.

When you finish, thank your Spirit Guides for their blessings and write down your experience.

Phoebe Garnsworthy

About the Author

Phoebe Garnsworthy is an Australian female author who loves to discover magic in everyday life. She has traveled the world extensively, exploring Eastern and Western philosophies alike, while studying the influences that these beliefs have on humanity.

The intention of her writing is to encourage conscious living and unconditional love.

www.PhoebeGarnsworthy.com
www.LostNowhere.com

Other books by Phoebe Garnsworthy

Lost Nowhere: A Journey of Self-Discovery (Book 1 of 2)
Lost Now Here: The Road to Healing (Book 2 of 2)
Daily Rituals: Positive Affirmations to Attract Love, Happiness & Peace

40915591R00060

Made in the USA
Middletown, DE
01 April 2019